Also published in Large Print from
G.K. Hall by T. V. Olsen:

Keno

T. V. Olsen

STARBUCK'S BRAND

G.K.HALL&CO.
Boston, Massachusetts
1992

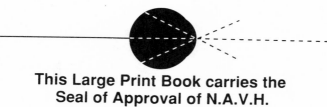

**This Large Print Book carries the
Seal of Approval of N.A.V.H.**

Copyright © 1973 by Theodore V. Olsen.

Published in Large Print by arrangement with
The Golden West Literary Agency.

G.K. Hall Large Print Book Series.

Printed on acid free paper in the United States of
America.

Set in 16 pt. Plantin.

Library of Congress Cataloging-in-Publication Data

Olsen, Theodore V.
    Starbuck's brand / T.V. Olsen.
       p. cm. — (G.K. Hall large print book series)
    ISBN 0-8161-5594-1
    1. Large type books. I. Title. II. Series.
[PS3565. L8S73 1992]
813'. 54 — dc20
                                   92-19929

Chapter 1

"Cut him loose," Perry said. "Then jump clear."

Just like that. Jed Starbuck looked at the mulberry-mottled calf hogtied on the ground, a crude *PJ* lettered in raw flesh on its flank. Then he raised his eyes to his brother.

That was Perry for you, Jed thought. His own gut was still tight from hearing the calf's pained bawl, smelling the singed hair and hide as Perry traced a straight iron over the animal's hip. Now his brother stood back with the smoking iron in his fist, as unconcerned as if he'd been putting on brands all his life.

Nothing ever seemed to faze Perry, and Jed knew it wasn't an act. Perry never had qualms and didn't understand why others had them. So he'd tossed out his follow-up order as casually as if he were commenting on the weather.

As a matter of fact, the weather was hot

enough to melt hell's hinges. But right now Jed figured that was the least of his worries. His whole body felt lacerated and beaten raw from tailing the young longhorn through the thorny chaparral. They'd finally boxed him in a tangle of mesquite; Perry had managed to throw a loop on him and drag him back to camp. Then had come the struggle of throwing him to the ground and tying his legs. They'd had no real idea of how to go about it.

Jed took off his battered hat and swiped a sleeve across his sweating face. He gazed briefly around their camp, set on a brushless flat dotted with sizable cottonwoods. Mesquite clung in pale green clouds to the horseshoe of shallow hills that circled the flat on three sides; on its fourth side, the Mora River crawled northwest to south like a thin looping snake. Sandbars jutting out like tawny tongues and the cottonwood and willow greenery high on the banks showed it had shrunk considerably in the summer dry. The Starbuck brothers had pitched camp just above the north bank, hobbling their three packhorses on the sparse grass. Two saddle mounts stood near the small branding fire, reins thrown, heads down. In a couple weeks they'd grown rib-gaunt; their coats were streaked with fresh scratches and dirty yellow froth.

No wonder the two riders at the line camp where they'd stopped yesterday had laughed their heads off. The brothers had thought the mounts they'd purchased from an Austin horsetrader were cowponies. "You boys got handed the wrong end of a taffy string," one had guffawed. "Them nags is gaited hunters." Perry's blue-green stare had turned wicked for a moment; then he'd given his easy laugh and said, "What's the difference?" In a few hours they'd picked up a small fund of knowledge on mustangs and how they were trained for cow work. The fact remained, Jed thought bleakly, that the Austin trader had foxed them like the greenhorns they were. And fatly overcharged them to boot.

"Get to it," Perry said. "Quit stalling."

"Who's stalling?"

Jed jerked his hat on, glaring defensively at his brother. He dredged only a thin comfort from the fact that for once, Perry cut an equally sorry figure beside him. Both were outfitted in range clothes that were all wrong for this country. Designed for northern ranges, not brushlands, they'd taken a beating. The broad hats kept getting lifted

3

off by brush; their jackets were torn at the sleeves, their batwing chaps scratched and ripped from getting hung up on brush and thorn. Jed's movements made dust powder whitely off his jacket except where it was muddied by great blotches of sweat. The back of his right pantsleg was torn from knee to cuff; a swinging horntip had snagged it and left a shallow slash on his calf. The faces and hands of both bore livid scratches. Perry had a bleeding cut under one eye; a flying hoof had grotesquely dented the crown of his hat. The two of them looked exactly as two damnfool Midwesterners deserved to look after being crazy enough to run down a wild *orejano* in the brambly thickets of the Texas *brasada*.

Jed opened the blade of his caseknife, bent down and carefully laid the keen edge against the thongs securing the yearling's legs. He wondered if hogtying didn't include a special knot of some kind that you could free with a yank, no cutting. This was a hell of a time to think of it.

He quickly cut the thongs and jumped back, but not fast or far enough. One of the freed calf's outlashing hind hoofs smashed him just below the right knee. Jed's leg buckled and he went down. The yearling sped

4

across the open, barreled into the dense mesquite and crashed away across a rise.

Perry stood looking after it. "That was it," he said, softly exultant. "That was the first one, Jedediah." He swung around and grinned down at Jed, who sat holding his knee. "Sorry as hell, boy. Really fetched you one, didn't he? Let's have a look at that."

"Don't bother," Jed snapped. "I don't expect I'll be laid up more than a week or so."

Sarcasm never touched Perry. He bent down, loosened Jed's chap and rolled up the torn pantsleg. He sighed and shook his head. "Christ, look at those clodhoppers! Why didn't you get some cowman's boots like I said?"

Jed rolled his toes comfortably in his thick-soled workshoes. "What in hell would I do with cowman's boots?"

"You'd ride better for one thing, the heel's for gripping stirrup."

"Yeah? I've tried yours. The toes are so damned tight, they're like to cripple a man."

"They'll break in."

Jed nodded glumly. "So will we if we don't get cut to dogmeat first."

Perry examined the mashed skin over his shinbone. "That's nothing. You can move it, can't you? I'll get the liniment."

He walked over to the cottonwood by which their gear was piled, limping a little in his pinch-toed boots. This is plain crazy, Jed thought. The whole goddam thing was crazy.

He'd thought the same from the time Perry had first come up with his big idea. They'd wasted enough of their lives grubbing away on a busted-down excuse for a farm. Perry had been reading about Southeast Texas; he'd talked to men who had been there. The Big Thicket was swarming with hundreds of thousands of cattle running wild and unbranded. Men claimed that a bummer with a cinch iron and a couple of sticks to hold it could brand himself rich. Those who got in early and staked their claims would be riding the crest one day. The beauty of it was, a man didn't need much to start off with. Just a meager outfit, a few riders and a pocket of land to work out from. The cattle were there for the taking.

Jed had argued heatedly. They didn't know a thing about the cattle game; they'd be complete greenhorns in a country full of seasoned men, a lot of whom might have the same idea. Perry had brushed the objections aside. "You don't know how big that country is, kid. Something like a quarter million square miles. Hardly any settlement at all between the Nueces and the Rio Grande rivers. As to experience, hell, all we need do is hire the right men; we can learn while we're building." So they had auctioned off the Ohio farm that was the sole legacy from their parents and had started for Texas . . .

Perry came back with the liniment. He uncorked the bottle and liberally slapped its contents on Jed's knee, ignoring his wincing grunts as it bit like fire into his raw flesh. "There. Tie a rag around it, you'll survive. I'll whip us up something to eat . . ."

Jed fished out a fairly clean bandanna and tied it around his knee. It would keep the pantsleg from chafing anyway. Perry dumped some beans in a Dutch oven, some coffee in a pot, added water to both and set them on the fire. Then he walked to the riverbank, peeling off his shirt. He knelt, splashed water on his head and torso, straightened up and toweled himself on his shirt.

Perry was big, but not bulky. He was tall and large-boned and long-muscled, his movements like a cat's. The sun gleamed on his wet yellow mane; he needed a haircut

7

and it lapped in tawny fantails over his ears and neck. His sun-boiled face was gaunt and squarish, a face that men could like and women did like; his broad expressive mouth shaped a grin that was wry and engaging. Jed always had a sense of something in leash about Perry, resources he'd never wholly tapped.

He knew that others felt it too. Perry had always been a leader with other fellows his age, leading them on all sorts of brawls and skylarkings. He'd gone into the war in '61 a private and had come out with a captain's bars. Perry never talked much about the war. He'd been wounded in November, 1864, outside of Nashville. His cavalry company had charged Chalmers's entrenched Rebel troops and he'd been shot from his saddle. The scar showed on the ropy compact muscles of his chest, a pale puckered circle the size of a silver dollar. When he turned, the much larger scar of the bullet's emergence was like an ugly fist-sized strawberry mark on the smooth skin of his back.

Jed never felt quite adequate beside him. He was nearly as tall as Perry, but loose-jointed and ungraceful, just starting to lose the gangling frame of youth. Jed's face was pugnosed and uninteresting. Except for his eyes, which were the sharp off-bleach color of all the Starbuck men's except Perry's; back in Ohio folks had always singled out a Starbuck by his eyes.

Perry ran against the mold that way as he did most every other way. His eyes weren't the ordinary brown of Ma's either. They were a rich blue-green, peculiarly bright, faintly challenging, full of strange kindling lights. But the strangeness went deeper. Perry was different. Always had been, even as a boy. His natural leadership accounted for some of it, as if his mother's quiet iron and his father's bombastic push had fused in him.

Perry returned to the fire, shrugging into his shirt. He squatted on his heels and grinned at Jed, then nodded around him. "Well, boy. What do you think of it?"

"You're serious, eh? This is the place?"

"Why'd you think we ran down that calf and branded him?"

Jed made a wry mouth. "I was wondering."

"That was just to sink our stake." Perry picked up the straight iron and drew letters in the dirt. *PJ.* "Our initials. Our spread. Our branded beef. That was the first, there'll be a thousand more. Then ten thousand."

He spoke very softly and Jed didn't laugh. It was Perry's dream; he was merely permitted to share it. He felt a quite uneasy reluctance that he couldn't wholly define.

Some of it, of course, stemmed from his first objections, which were richly borne out during the journey south. They'd traveled by riverboat to St. Louis, by stage to Austin. There they had banked the proceeds of the farm sale and had outfitted themselves for the plain. There too they'd been mulcted by the horsetrader, which was their second blunder if you counted coming to this country as the first.

A couple rugged weeks on horseback had brought them deep into the *brasada*. Sun-baked savannahs and vast copses of tangled chaparral. Brown water and black thorn and miles of mesquite-stippled waste. And grass too, as Perry had said. A million acres of tough Texas grass whose roots reached deep into the earth and squeezed out every hidden drop of moisture. And cattle, yes, there must be hundreds of thousands of them, multicolored longhorns of every conceivable shade: black, white, brown, red, buff, blue, speckled and streaky, with a kind of faded-rust hue predominating. Spanish cattle, bred and rebred for generations till a man couldn't roll over in his sleep without spooking up a dozen.

Perry had been right on a second count. In this year of 1867, the region was little-settled. Here and there were one-loop outfits belonging to Mexican brushpoppers, a handful of others run by equally hard-scrabble Americans. There were a very few large spreads dominated by old Spanish families The line shack they'd stopped at yesterday belonged, the riders had told them, to Major Troy Hobart's TH outfit, the only really sizable Anglo outfit in the whole area. "By God, this is man's country," Perry had enthused. To Jed, it seemed a desolate and Godforsaken piece of creation . . .

"This trip is just a preliminary," Perry was saying. "We came looking for choice land. We've found it." He picked up a handful of tan earth and juggled it in his palm. "We'll build our headquarters here. A house under those trees. A bunkhouse on that rise of land yonder. Barns over there. Corrals stretching along the river . . ."

Jed gingerly rubbed his sunburned neck. "What about a crew? We'll need riders with the kind of know-how we sure as hell don't have."

"We'll find 'em."

"Then there's the Act of '66," Jed said acidly. "Do you plan to repeal it?"

Perry flicked a grin. They'd learned about the Act of '66 while in Austin. An act rammed through by big Texas cowmen who'd built their own fortunes by mavericking. Anyone caught trailing even unbranded stock off its native range was liable to fine and imprisonment. Worse, if he got caught by private parties.

"It's as I said before, kid. We're in South Texas below the Nueces now. Damned little settlement and damned little law. Not enough hereabouts to put in a *ladino*'s eye."

"I'd imagine there's a local or two that might not take kindly to hot-iron artists on their land either."

Perry merely grunted.

They'd hashed it all out before. Perry had checked a lot of maps and old records up in Austin; he'd copied some of the maps and brought them along. As he reckoned it, there was no title on this particular piece except an old Spanish crown grant made out to a Don Felipe Aguara y Parral in the late 1700s. "Once I've consolidated my holdings, I'll go about establishing title," Perry had said con-

12

fidently. "Money, influence. That's all it'll take. And I'll have them. A man can grow in wide-open country like this, Jed. Grow as big as he wants. He can be his own law. All he needs is the guts to make it stick."

Jed was handicapped trying to argue with him. Perry was eight years older; he'd "seen the elephant" everywhere from Chicago to St. Louis. Jed, who barely topped legal age, had hardly been anywhere or seen anything, a deficiency of which he was keenly aware. Besides he'd idolized Perry as a kid, and though he was old enough to know better, some habits were hard to break. Then, Perry was partly right. The farm in Ohio had been a poor bet. It would have taken long grinding years just to work off the debts the Old Man had accumulated, much less make the place a paying proposition . . .

Suddenly Perry was on his feet. He walked unhurriedly toward their pile of gear, his eyes fixed on a rise flanking the west side of the flat. Jed followed his glance. Two men were sitting their horses there. They'd ridden up quietly from behind the rise.

Jed's immediate thought was that they weren't here by chance. Not coming up on the camp like that, hidden from sight till they

13

were almost on top of it, then just sitting up there and looking on. Jed got to his feet. Where had these men come from?

Perry picked up the two rifles leaning against the other gear, both Army Springfields. He tossed one to Jed. The two riders came slowly down the incline and across the flat, halting some ten yards off.

"Good afternoon, señores," said the younger one.

"Light down," Perry said.

"No, *mil gracias.*" The young man flipped a gloved hand, indicating the camp. "You have camped here a night, I am told. Will you be here another night?"

Perry was silent for ten seconds, studying him. He was a bony-whiplash of a youth with a thin handsome olive-skinned face and a hairline mustache. He sat his black horse with an almost feminine grace; his lips were full, fluted like the edge of a tart, faintly cruel. He wore fancy-braided clothes and his beautifully tooled saddle was heavy with silver trim.

"We planned on it," Perry said.

"And then?"

"We might leave."

"Ah."

"For a time." Perry shifted the rifle barrel

14

resting in the crook of his left arm. "We plan to be back."

"Ah." The rider was shaking his head, smiling slightly, before Perry was through speaking. "A night, two nights. That's permitted. But longer, no. And to come back, no."

"We're going to live here," Perry said quietly.

"Señior. You are on the land of Don Solano Diego y Parral. I am his son, Augustin. This is my *segundo,* Tito Rozales. In my father's name, I bid you welcome. Until tomorrow at this time."

"Then?"

Jed felt a thickening uneasiness. He had seen the same cold light in Perry's eyes before and he knew what it meant. You could push hell and high water at him and it wouldn't matter.

Young Parral gazed at him a moment, then swung his hand in a half-circle. "All the land south of this river to a distance of twenty miles. All the land north to a distance of ten—"

"East to twenty miles and west another twenty," Perry said.

Parral's black eyes were inexpressive. "For a hundred years our family has held this land

15

on a grant from the King of Spain. These grants have been honored in your American courts."

"Sometimes," Perry retorted.

"All this is Parral land. All the *cimarrones* and *ladinos* and *orejanos* on it are Parral cattle." Nodding at the rifle and ropes and straight iron. "Have you branded any?"

"One. We're going to brand a lot more."

Parral smiled. "I think you are wrong, señor."

He gave a long sharp whistle. Two more riders came up into view on the rise. When the brothers looked toward them, Parral said, "And behind you, señores."

Another pair of *vaqueros* rode out of the thick mesquite beyond the cottonwoods. Two others came onto the bank across the river and splashed through the muddy shallows and up the near bank, halting just behind Jed and Perry. All had rifles out, held ready.

"*Mañana* seems a long way off," Parral said. "The closest Parral boundary is to the north. So you do not lose your way, we will show you to it now."

"I guess you came prepared for it," murmured Perry.

"'Yesterday a *vaquero* saw your camp and

16

came at once to the *hacienda*. It is a long way and we do not do things in a rush like you *Yanquis*. Don Solaao desired that I should be polite but also bring men in case your understanding was slow. Now, *andale* —I have always wondered how fast a *Yanqui* who understands slow can move."

Perry smiled. "It's about as far to your *hacienda* as to the north line, eh?"

"Es verdad. And so?"

"Maybe I can save your men some time." Perry tipped his rifle quickly up. "They won't have to ride half so far, just taking Don Solano back his son's body."

Parral gazed down the blued barrel pointed at his belly. *"Por Dios.* I think you are mad."

"Tell your men to pull off. Then we'll talk."

"And this one—" Parral's pointed glance touched Jed. "He has a desire to die with you?"

"And you," Perry said flatly.

Jed looked around at the *vaqueros*. "I think we're between a rock and a hard place," he said, making his voice calm. He was gut-tight, hot trickles of sweat gliding down his ribs. He knew Perry too well; there was no limit to Perry's game.

Jed had to make a decision and he made it. He threw his rifle to the ground.

"He is not so quick to meet death. Now—señor?"

The cold stubbornness froze Perry's face. He thumbed back the Springfield's hammer, a rasping sound that ended in the roar of a shot. It didn't come from the Springfield.

The slug's force knocked Perry spinning. He hit the ground on his back and lay clutching his blood-pumping thigh with both hands.

"*Gracias,* Uvalde," Partal smiled at the *vaquero* who'd fired. "But at such a range you should shoot a pig dead. *Es nada.* I will show you how to skin a living one."

He lifted a whip coiled around the flat heavy horn of his saddle. Shook it out. A nine-foot leaded muleskinner's whip, sinuous as a blacksnake. He cracked it once, the tip snapping up a puff of dust.

Jed clenched his fists. "You can't!" he yelled. "You can't do this!"

Parral laughed.

"Augustin." Tito Rozales reined close to him, laying a hand like a brown ham on his arm. The *segundo* was huge and barrel-bodied, jowled like a prize hog. "Is enough,"

18

he said in labored English, for the Starbucks' benefit. "Let them be. We take them across line. They will not come back."

"This one? Look at him, Tito. Look."

Perry had rolled onto his side, raising himself on one elbow. His eyes blazed with a chill hatred.

"When he comes again," Parral said, "we will have to kill him. We do not know who he is, what friends he has. Maybe that would bring a *Yanqui* marshal. So, Tito. *¡Tormemos del mal el menos!*"

He stepped his horse forward and sent the whip furling out. Perry moved with surprising vitality, rolling his body over. The tip cut his sleeve and left a streak of blood. Grunting, he floundered up on his hands and knees. Parral swung, flicking the lash expertly across his back, splitting his shirt open.

Perry yelled in pain.

Somehow he stumbled to his feet and lunged at Parral's stirrup. His leg gave way and he pitched down. Another blow fell on his back. Parral danced his horse around the fallen man, his lips fluting back off his teeth. Perry got up, more slowly this time, gripping his thigh with one hand as he tried to swing around and face Parral.

19

The lash cut him across the shoulders. Perry grabbed at it, but it snaked across his palm and free. It whirred back for another stroke. Perry wheeled and took a lurching step away as the whip shot out. It curled around his head with a fleshy snap.

Perry shouted and plunged back on his hands and knees. Blood spurted from his nose and forehead. Again he crawled to his feet. Again the whip sliced out and broke flesh.

Jed stood locked with horror. Now he made a move and instantly felt the cold touch of a *vaquero*'s rifle muzzle on the back of his neck.

Perry kept falling and getting up, staggering in blind circles now, as the whip caught him again and again. In seconds his clothes were flapping in bloody strips; blood streamed from cuts over his whole body.

"Stop it!" Jed's voice was a thin scream. "Stop it, goddam you!"

Parral pulled his mount up, reining him around toward Jed. His face was glistening, his teeth pulled back.

"*Basta*, Augustin! *¡Basta!*" Tito Rozales crowded his horse against Parral's and this time caught his hand in a grip like a vise.

Perry was climbing to his feet once more.

His face was a grotesque jellied mask of blood and dirt. He took five looping bent-over steps, fell on the sloping bank and tumbled down it into the shallow water. He lay on his back, heaving and twitching like a half-grounded fish.

"Now," Parral said, coiling his whip, "you have paid for the cow, gringo. It is yours."

Chapter 2

Parral eyed Jed for some seconds, as if he were undecided. Finally he nodded at Perry. "What is he to you?"

"My brother," Jed said thickly.

"Your brother is a fool," Parral said. "Next time he is a dead fool, *sabe?* We will be back tomorrow. You must be gone from here. We will track you clear to our line and you must be across it."

He swung his black and put him across the muddy shallows of the Mora at a brisk trot. His *vaqueros* fell in behind him. Tito Rozales hung back; he looked at Jed.

"Is no good for you here," he said. "You are the cool head, you see this. Your brother, he better see it too. You know what a horse drag look like? Injun kind?" His slablike hands made vague motions. "The travois?"

Jed nodded.

"You make one for your brother. I do not think he ride for a long time. Here, look." Rozales pointed. "That way is an Anglo ranch. Is ten mile straight north. You got compass?"

"Yes."

"Is straight north, you cannot miss. There is a place north-west called Moratown with the doctor, but is thirty mile. The rancher's name, it is Hobart. You go there."

Rozales rode after his companions.

Jed seemed to rouse from a trance. He trudged over to where Perry lay. His brother was nearly unconscious. The bloody shreds of his clothes clung wetly to the raw stripes that covered his torso. The blows had caught him with bruising welting force even where they hadn't split the skin. His face was purpling, lopsidedly swollen, several ugly cuts angling across his face. The side of his mouth had been laid open and a patch of skin dangled over one eyebrow.

Somehow his lips forced speech. "Got . . . to get . . . bullet out. Do that . . . first."

Jed caught him under the arms and dragged him up the bank to the shade of a large cottonwood. Then he cut away the blood-soaked pantsleg. Perry's thigh was a mess where the bullet had gone in, a worse mess where it had come out. It had missed the bone. But a leg was more than bone. It was flesh and nerves and blood vessels. A lead ball almost a half-inch across flattening as it passed through literally pulverized it.

Jed straightened up. He stared at the shroud of dust tailing after the Parral riders. *Those goddam . . . goddam greasers.* The word was dredged from his dim childhood. There were no Mexicans in Ohio, but men who'd fought in the Mexican War had always called them "greasers."

Perry raised his head, his neck muscles straining. Jed bent down to catch his words. "Get . . . bullet out."

"It went clean through, Perr."

"Get . . . iron. Stick it back . . . in fire."

Jed licked his lips. "I—I don't know if I can do it."

"I . . . been shot . . . before. You . . . do it."

Perry's head fell back. Jed went to the fire and picked up the straight iron. He cleaned it off as well as he could, then thrust it into the coals.

With nobody to help hold Perry down, the

only way Jed could manage the cauterizing was by sitting on his brother's legs. He dabbed the iron on with touch-on-touch cautery, as he'd seen done with animals. At first Perry's body quivered and heaved under him, and then he went limp. The rest of the job would have been easy except for the smell of burned flesh and the fact that his own throat was burning with a rise of stomach juices. Somehow he finished cauterizing both openings of the wound. Then he went off a little way and threw up.

He was shaking, his clothes soaked with sweat. All right, that was the worst, he thought. Now you can finish it up. Go on, move.

He inspected the raw welts on Perry's torso; his own flesh crawled. The whip's leaded tip must have lifted coin-sized pieces of skin partly off wherever it landed. Augustin Parral had the touch of an artist. Jed tied the leg up with a spare shirt of his, then unlashed the soogan rolls from their saddles and spread them out. He cut away and peeled off the remains of Perry's clothing and eased him onto the blanket. The touch of hands and rough fabric on his tortured flesh must have caused exquisite agony, but he never let out a sound.

"Perry—"

"Salve . . . in bag. Get it . . ."

Jed rummaged through Perry's saddle-bags and found a small flat can labeled DR. BENEDICT'S MAGIC GILEAD BALM. A CURE FOR ALL AILMENTS TO WHICH THE FLESH IS HEIR. Which meant everything from gall sores to colic. He began smearing the tarry ointment over Perry's lacerated body, feeling him shudder and jerk. God, he needed sewing up in a dozen places. Perry lay with his teeth clenched, eyes wide open and fierce with pain.

"You need doctoring," Jed told him. "The fat one said Hobart's ranch is ten miles due north. That would be about where those fellows at the line shack yesterday said it was."

"You ride . . . there. Bring help."

"Perry, we've got to get clear away from here. That Parral . . . he said he'd be back tomorrow. Said he'd track us clear to their line. What I'll do is make a horse drag to carry you."

Perry didn't reply. Jed started to turn away and Perry's husky voice stopped him: "You hadn't . . . thrown away . . . your gun . . . we might have . . . bluffed 'em off."

Jed stared at him. "You can't believe that!"

25

Perry's mouth puckered in a gruesome grin. "No . . . I guess not."

Jed got the hand ax and prowled along the riverbank till he'd located a couple of tall straight saplings which he cut down, limbed off and top-trimmed, making two fifteen-foot poles. He cut his rawhide *riata* into lengths and used them to secure his ground-sheet on crosspieces between the poles. He made the poles fast to Perry's saddle, covered him with a blanket and tied him loosely down.

Though only half aware of what was happening, Perry fought to squeeze back sounds of pain. Sweat stood in red drops on his torn face. He had the guts of a tiger, but whipped to a jelly as he was, he'd need a lot more.

Jed loaded their plunder on the pack-horses and diamond-hitched the loads securely. He tied the packhorses together on a single line and fastened it to the travois. Then he took a bearing with Perry's compass, mounted his gaited hunter and pushed north through the brush, leading the other horses.

The sun's brassy ball looped past midafternoon, the orange sear of light hot and blinding. Jed canted his hatbrim against it and rode doggedly on, stopping often to check his compass. He wanted to hold a straight course to the Parral boundary, wherever the hell that was, and of course to the Hobart ranch headquarters. That was the tricky part. Straight north. But it would be terrifyingly easy to miss, even so. No fences or line markers in this great hellsmear of a country. Hard to reckon distance on a dun-colored landscape corrugated into bland hills that were useless as landmarks, yet cut off your view so completely that you might blunder any time into rambling clots of mesquite and chaparral. It forced a lot of awkward detours. One thing sure, they wouldn't cover any ten miles before dark . . .

The sun sank west like a swollen orange. Jed needed rest and so did the horses. He could only guess at what Perry was enduring, every scrape and jounce of the drag across the uneven ground tearing at his raw and lacerated body. Time to stop. They hadn't covered five miles, but they could get some sleep and start out again when it was light enough to see.

Jed made camp in a shallow swale, piled up some dead mesquite and built a fire. He divided the water of one canteen between the Dutch oven and the coffeepot, boiled up beans and half-chicory coffee and wolfed them down. Perry didn't have much appetite, but managed to swallow a cup of water and eat a biscuit. He was fully conscious now, sweating with the pain he kept biting back. He lay beside the fire covered against the night cool by a single blanket, all that his pain-wracked body could tolerate.

The last daylight faded; inky shadows pooled outside the firelight. Jed spread out his soogans and tried to compose himself for sleep. He forced his muscles to relax, but his mind wouldn't. It kept prowling restlessly over the events of the day. Twice he nearly dozed off, only to jerk awake. First from the luting of a horned owl, then the cutting wail of a coyote.

This country wasn't for him, he thought. He liked his nature tamed, curried, and cultivated. You heard owls and coyotes in Ohio too, but their voices never had the raw wild significance they carried here.

A thought struck him. A question. Oddly it hadn't occurred to him till now . . . and knowing Perry, he should have asked it. He glanced toward his brother. He was still awake.

"Perr."

"Yeah?"

"What do we do now?"

"What we set out to do." Perry's pulpy face turned toward him. His eyes were bright and hard. "We came to stake out some land."

"Not that piece, though. Not now."

"That piece. Not now, but damned soon."

"You know, Perr? That Parral fellow said you're a fool. He's wrong. You're not a fool. You're plain crazy."

"Think so, Jed boy?"

"You just got your life halfway beat out of you," Jed almost yelled, "and it didn't teach you anything!"

Perry grinned. "I came a long way to find what I wanted . . . back there by the Mora. You think some whip-snapping spick dandy is going to stop me?"

"Perr, for God's sake! What'll stop you next time is cold lead!"

"Next time I'll have my odds properly sized. And prepare accordingly."

"What do you mean?"

"Don't you fret about it. I'm green, I admit it. But I learn fast. You know that."

"God! I wonder."

"Listen, kid." Perry's sea-colored eyes glinted wickedly. "You've wondered why there aren't others down in this country with my ideas. Men with money, men with experience. I'll tell you why. It's a matter of guts. Simple guts. The vital ingredient. I'm gambling, I don't deny it. I haven't as much to lose as some, but that's not the point. I'll stake all I have—"

"And all I have?"

"You can deal your half out any time. You want to?"

Jed shook his head bitterly. "I don't know. I just never bargained for anything like this."

Perry smiled at the sky. "Well, kid, we're different that way. Me, this is what I've been looking for. A wide-open game in a wide-open country. Let the little men of the world play it safe. Hard work and ambition are only part of it. The rest is guts. The willingness to take a naked gamble. The stakes, your life. Or an empire. That's what it's all about, Jed. That's the heart of the game.

Jed groaned wearily. He rolled over and put his back to Perry. After a time, he slept . . .

When false dawn began to gray the land, Jed roused himself and had a look at Perry's leg. A little crusted blood on the bandage, not much. The cautery had taken all right. But the leg and scabbed-over cuts needed some competent attention and soon. Perry was burning with fever, shiny-eyed and mumbling, starting to go out of his head. Jed got him back on the travois, broke camp and began trekking north again.

Sunup. An explosion of pink and gold flattened along a rippled black cut-out of horizon. They had come another five miles, Jed guessed, rubbing a hand over his slightly whiskered jaw. The hand trembled with fatigue. Keep going, he thought. And hope to hell they hadn't run way off course, what with twisting this way and that around brush mottes. Noon. If they didn't raise the Hobart place by noon, they'd gone wrong somewhere . . .

Midmorning. Hearing a crash of brush ahead of him, Jed halted the horses.

An instant later, a big brindle *ladino* came surging out of the mesquite and quartered away to their right. Then a rider pulled into view, tailing the brindle.

Seeing them, he reined up.

"Well, I'm a som bitch," he said. "Ain' that som'thing."

Jed stared at him through a film of exhaustion. He saw an obvious Mexican wearing *taja* leggings and an embroidered jacket, and the panicked thought came to him that this was a Parral rider. The Mexican was a short man, hard and trim and finely knit, and he sat his saddle with a big man's easy poise. His face was long and lantern-jawed with a nose like a blade, thickened from being broken once or twice.

"Is this Parral land?" Jed's voice was a parched croak.

"Naw, she's Hobart land." The rider gave a toothy yellow smile that made his ugly face suddenly comical and likable. "You got the trouble, hey?"

"Yeah." Jed felt his body sag slightly, as if some tension had run out of it. "My brother needs help. Can you tell me where . . . ?"

The Mexican turned his head and cupped his hands around a shout. "Aaron! Hey, Aaron!" Then he reined over by the travois and dismounted. He looked at Perry's face and whistled. "Ho boy, ain' that a som bitch, though. Who do this to him?"

"A dirty. . ." Jed swallowed. "A man named Parral."

The Mexican whistled again. "Ho boy, you grab yourself a sack of hell, I'm think."

A man on a chesty grulla came riding into view. He was gaunt-limbed and big-jointed in a *brasadero* rig of stout leather jacket, narrow chaps and small-brimmed hat. His hands were like scarred hams, his legs so long that the stirrups were set inches below the grulla's barrel. His saddle-colored face was all knobs and hollows, mastiff-jawed, and he had a look of authority.

"I'm Jed Starbuck," said Jed. "This is my brother Perry. He needs help."

"Aaron Troop," the big man said. "Range boss for Major Hobart." He nodded at the Mexican. "Leandro Mirabel here." He stepped out of his saddle and walked over to the travois. He didn't just stand, he towered. Jed, who was six feet even, felt dwarfed.

"Looks like he argufyed with a whole flock of wowsers and lost," Troop said. He glanced at Mirabel. "Leandro, you ride back to the *casa*. Tell the Major to have Miss Beth or Ceferina fix up a room and bed. Then fetch the buckboard far as Tuley Spring. It ain't over a mile from here and we won't get no wagon into this brush."

With Troop leading the way, they cut northwest through the mesquite and chaparral. The country began to open up: more grass and less brush. Tuley Spring was a pan-shaped seep bordered by willows and a wallow of trampled mud. It was the main waterhole on their range, Aaron Troop said, and pretty near central to it. Come cowhunt time, the riders always worked out from here. There were a few cottonwoods to keep the sun off. While they waited, Troop examined Perry's leg and the worst of his cuts.

"Some crackerjack with a whip do this?"

Jed nodded dismally. "Augustin Parral was his name."

"That so?" Troop's pale blue eyes prodded his face. "You boys trespassing?"

Jed told him how it had happened.

"Yeh." Troop rubbed his chin. "That Augustin is a mean little rat. Tito Rozales keeps him in line most times or somebody'd of blowed his head off long while ago. You boys Yankees, eh?"

"We're from Ohio."

"Jee-*zus*," Troop muttered.

It was past high noon. Jed squatted exhaustedly in the cottonwood shade, feeling completely drained. It was an effort to answer Troop's spare, prodding questions. A road of sorts snaked away from the spring across a north flat and Jed kept his eyes on it. Finally he saw a wagon coming along it, furling up a ribbon of dust. In a few minutes Leandro Mirabel reined up by the spring.

"Miss Beth, she is get set up for the hurt

one," he said. "She wan' to com' here with me, but the Major, he say no, the sun he is raise planty hob with her comple'sion. Wha's comple'sion, Aaron?"

"Skin."

"Why in hell ain' he say so?"

They loaded Perry into the spring bed of the buckboard; Jed and Aaron Troop jogged behind it as they headed down the road.

"Miss Beth," Jed said. "Would she be Mrs. Hobart?"

"Naw. Miss Elizabeth's the Major's only child." Troop removed his hat and mopped his forehead with a bandanna; his hair was so close-cropped, his skull resembled a blond burr. "All she got to hear is some waddy took a thorn in his toe and she is rushing to put a nice clean bandage on it. Got this mangy crew spoilt rotten."

The road wound through a jag of hills which ended in a wide grass flat where the TH headquarters lay. The *casa grande,* as Troop called it, a rambling one-story whitewashed building with an adobe enclosure at one side, was set in a belt of big old cottonwoods. Beyond it was a long dun-colored adobe that looked like a combination cookshack and bunkhouse; a tangle of barns, sheds and pole corrals stretched across a grassless hard-packed area to the east. Set off by itself a distance from the house was a small, crumbling, distinctively Mexican chapel with its cross and bell.

"Looks like a greaser place," Jed said without thinking.

"Major bought it off a Mex family." Troop's glance was stone-cold. "You want to watch how you call Mexican folks hereabouts. Major, he fit 'em back in '46, but he don't take kindly to some Texican, and I might add Yankee, notions. Half our crew is Mex."

They rode through a gateway in the adobe wall into a flagstoned patio. Two people stepped out of a doorway. One was man in his shirtsleeves, fanning himself with a palm-leaf fan. The other was a woman in her early twenties.

Jed was awed. She was about the loveliest creature he had ever seen. Long-legged slender, as tall as most men. A cool sculptured beauty that was almost regal. She wore a green frock that matched her eyes; a wide straw hat with a green ribbon rode her thick-piled auburn hair and half-shaded her face. Cream and rose-ivory skin. He guessed sun would raise holy hell, all right, with a skin like that.

He stepped stiffly down; Troop made the introductions. Major Troy Hobart was a stocky whittle-hipped man in his mid-fifties with a spade beard and a stiff shock of pepper-and-salt hair to match. He had a crisp voice and dry manner; humor meshed the sun-crinkled skin at the corners of his eyes with deep sly lines. He had a good firm grip and Miss Elizabeth's hand clasp was cool and ladylike.

She walked to the wagon and looked into the spring bed. She was very brisk. "How do you do, Mr. Starbuck?"

Perry's cracked mouth managed a weak but engaging grin. "However I look, ma'am, I am enchanted."

"Indeed? I'll try not to disenchant you. But you'll need sewing on those face cuts. And perhaps elsewhere. We'll see." She turned her head. "Ceferina!"

A heavy Mexican woman flat-footed to the doorway. "Yes'm?"

"Get out my sewing box and bring it to the room we've prepared. And some soap and hot water too. We'll have to clean him up first."

Perry's smile faded. "See here, you can't . . ."

"I had two brothers," Elizabeth Hobart

said. "Had. Both died fighting your Yankee invaders. Also I've seen men drunk, dead, and in every shade of condition between. So don't drag out your manly modesty for me, Mr. Starbuck. It'll be wasted, I assure you."

Chapter 3

"Where do you fellows hail from?" Major Hobart asked pleasantly.

"Ohio," Troop said dourly. "They're from Ohio."

"It's not a bad word, Aaron," Elizabeth smiled. "You'd have a hard time finding an Anglo-Texican whose Texas roots go back more than two generations, ours included. Are you sure you've had enough to eat, Mr. Starbuck?"

Jed was so stuffed that he wondered if he'd ever move again. "Yes'm. Yes, indeed."

He couldn't have very well turned down the Hobarts' gracious invitation to supper, so he'd slicked and curried himself up the best way he could. But his horse-smelling clothes and rather abashed feeling made him out of place in this genteel candlelit room. It was largely occupied by a fine oak table that had been freighted in from somewhere, covered with white damask and centered by a silver candlepiece. All the tableware was silver, the dishes good china. None of which kept him from doing justice to a good meal of fried chicken, barbecued beef, red-eyed beans, potatoes, greens, cornbread, and apple pie washed down by a quart or so of good coffee. It was like manna after weeks of living on beans, hardtack that was almost impervious to teeth, half-chicory coffee full of grounds that you strained out through your teeth.

The Major nodded his white head. "Beth's right, Aaron. But it gets harder to remember that we're natives of Virginia." He rose, walked to the mammoth walnut sideboard and rummaged about. "Where are those damned Havanas?"

"At your elbow, Father," said Elizabeth.

She looked very lovely and cool in a dress of pale blue satin that set off her ivory skin. Candlelight touched fiery glints on her hair. A polite and quiet lady, but all the same, as Jed had seen, she ran the Hobart household with a firmly efficient hand. After he and Leandro Mirabel had carried Perry to the room prepared for him, they'd been ushered out. Major Hobart had assured Jed that

Perry couldn't be in better hands with a bonafide sawbones. Elizabeth had been away at school in Richmond, Virginia, when the war began; she'd organized a batch of school chums into a corps of volunteer nurses to care for wounded soldiers. Presently she'd come out to tell them that with a few weeks' rest, Perry should be as fit as ever.

The Major held out a humidor. "Mr. Starbuck?"

"No, sir, thank you."

Troop accepted a cigar, and Hobart went on: "Came out as an Austin colonist myself. Never left Texas again except during the war. Led a bunch of volunteers in the 2nd Texas Infantry. Fought at Iuka, Farmington, Shiloh, Vicksburg. Captured there and released to go home on giving my parole. Were you in the war, Mr. Starbuck?"

"No, sir. I was too young when it started, and somebody had to help Pa with the farm. Perry joined up right away. He was wounded at Nashville."

The Major nodded dryly. "Nashville, eh? I wasn't there, but quite a few Texans were." He picked up the candelabra and lighted Troop's cigar, then his own. "If you'll forgive my curiosity, exactly what the devil are you two doing clear down in the *brasada* trying to start off something you know nothing about? And why did Augustin Parral work your brother over with a whip?"

Jed told him the whole story.

The Major's fine mouth twisted with disgust. "That young Parral is a devil. Hard on his horses and his women, they say. Not the man his father is . . . though I don't know any of them well except the daughter. She visits occasionally—friend of Elizabeth's." He looked keenly at Jed. "I hope your brother doesn't intend to pursue this venture any further."

"He's more set on it than ever, sir."

"But not to settle on Parral land—eh?"

"Right smack on the same place. He said so."

"Thunderation," muttered the Major. "We'll have to try to talk him out of that. Interesting. A beating like that one should have knocked all the sand out of him. Apparently it didn't."

"He's a strange man," Elizabeth murmured.

"That doesn't say the half," Troop grunted. "Other half is, he's plain crazy."

The Major puffed his Havana reflectively. "In a way I sympathize with Solano Parral.

Not with what that whelp of his did, that was inexcusable. But his people were here when our people were still British subjects on the eastern side of the Appalachians. They brought in the horses and the cattle, they fought Indians and they Christianized 'em. Tamed all the land we've taken from 'em and built a unique culture on it. This is their last real stronghold on United States soil and knowing they hold it—in the long run—on American sufferance pinks their pride, of which they've plenty. They're sensitive as hell about intruders."

"They don't look on you as one, sir?" Jed asked.

"Very likely. But with a difference. The Austin government offered me a headright league of land for my services in the Mexican War, but I declined the offer. I had independent means and preferred to start out on my own on land of my choice. Bought this place from the Archuletas, a once-wealthy family who'd fallen on bad times, paid 'em a fair price. Told all my neighbors, big and little, Mexican and Anglo alike, that I'd never extend myself any direction beyond the original boundaries. I've kept that promise. Don Solano knows our common boundary as established by the old crown grants will never be contested by me. We get along. Throw our crews together for joint cowhunts sometimes."

"We could push out a good ways if we had a mind to," Troop observed.

Hobart chuckled out a cloud of smoke. "Now, yes. We've argued it before, Aaron— stick to what's' yours in terms of hard agreement. In time others will come: Legitimate claimants with Spanish grants, Mexican grants, headright claims. Iron artists of every stripe. They'll end up at each other's throats. How much does it take to satisfy a man? I can't answer for anyone else. My grandfather had an estate in the north of England. My father developed a plantation in the Tidewater three times as large. I have a domain as absolute as either of theirs and larger by far. I can afford to fight for it, would if need be, but I wouldn't count it worth the candle to squabble over even one acre more."

"Won't you have more coffee, Mr. Starbuck?" Elizabeth asked.

"No'm. Thank you."

The Major gazed at the tablecloth, his steepled thumbs grooving his underlip. "Your brother is going to be laid up a long time. Meantime you're at loose ends. Cowhunt time is coming up, I always hire extra hands around then. How would you like to hire onto my crew?"

"Major, why take on a completely green hand?" Troop asked dourly.

"And Yankee," Elizabeth said dryly. "You say it even when you don't, Aaron."

"War's over," the Major said brusquely. "Time we let the dead rest."

Troop shrugged. "Your outfit. The men might have some strong feelings on it. All I'm saying, he's greener'n spring grass."

"Everyone was green once, Aaron. Even you. Let him start at the bottom, everyone does." Hobart looked at Jed. "Well, are you interested? Thirty a month, bed and board. If you're going to stay in this country, you'll find the experience invaluable."

"I'd have to . . ." Jed broke off, embarrassed. Why ask Perry when it was rightly his decision? "Yes, sir. That sounds fine."

"I'll talk to your brother as well. Maybe he'll hire on when he's able."

Troop snorted quietly. "Major, all this Samaritan stuff won't get a herd to market."

Hobart laughed. "Call it an investment in the general weal. Both these fellows seem quick, smart, well-spoken. I'd guess they've had education beyond the average. Am I right, boy?"

44

"Perry attended an agricultural school," Jed said. "The war broke off his education. I had a year of normal school and I taught country school for a year after Pa died and before Perry came back from the war. Then we both returned to the family farm and tried to get it back on a paying basis."

"And you couldn't, eh? Why not?"

"Debts."

The Major considerately didn't press for details. "I'm gambling you're a pair of hard workers who've had poor luck. Aaron, what I'm saying is that Texas is broken and impoverished, she wants new ambition, new blood. She needs young men like these two. If I can give them a start, all to the good. I'll expect you to help break 'em in . . . and to ease their way into the crew."

"If I didn't know you better, Major, I'd swear you want 'em coddled."

"Not what I mean and you know it. Most of the boys on the crew fought for Texas. Your attitude could make a difference."

Troop gave a noncommittal grunt.

Jed said that if he was going to work here, he'd better move his things to the bunkhouse tonight. He excused himself and went to the room that Elizabeth had assigned to him earlier. All he had to do was pick up his blanketroll and saddlebags; their larger gear had already been stored in the bunkhouse.

Before leaving, he looked in on Perry in the adjoining bedroom. A low-turned lamp burned on the commode; Perry was asleep in the big fourposter, the blankets pulled to his chin. The white bandage around his forehead looked startling against his ruddy skin. His face had a saffron tinge, but maybe that was only the light. He seemed to be resting comfortably. Jed tiptoed out, closed the door and passed through the parlor, pausing to say good night to the Major and thank him for the job.

"It's just an opportunity, boy," Hobart said. "You'll have to show what you're made of. Good night."

As Jed stepped out into the dark patio, he saw two figures walking in the shadows beside the south wall. A beam of windowlight touched Elizabeth's blue dress; the towering form beside her was Aaron Troop. His head was bent almost possessively toward her as they quietly talked.

Jed felt a nudge of surprise. Troop might be the Hobarts' range boss, might even share their table now and then, but he seemed out of his element. He was a big rough sort and Miss Elizabeth was quality, a lady; but somehow this didn't pinpoint the jarring note Jed felt in seeing them together.

Well, it was none of his business.

He left the patio and crossed the trampled lot to the cookshack-bunkhouse. Lights showed in the greased-paper windows. Jed fumbled for the latch of the puncheon door and entered the storeroom, a ten-by-twenty area filled with old hide trunks and the crew's spare gear, including his and Perry's. Idle voices and the strains of a whining harmonica came through the doorway beyond. It led to the bunkroom.

A kind of reserved quiet descended on the room, dim with tobacco smoke, as Jed stepped into it. There were ten sets of double bunks, most of them in use. A potbelly stove centered the room; a table beside it was littered with well-worn magazines and newspapers. On the table lay an open volume that Jed recognized; a Dutch Almanac with Thedford Black Draught advertising. Every farm home had one, and apparently so did every ranch.

Some of the men were sprawled in their bunks, reading by the fitful light of a big coal oil lamp suspended by a wire from the ceiling. Others sat on their bunks mending clothes, playing cards or shooting the bull.

Everyone looked at Jed. None of them showed any particular reaction, but he noticed that each man studied him head to foot, sizing up his clothes. Their stares held longest on his heavy shoes. The only man he knew was Leandro Mirabel. At least half the others were Mexicans too.

"I'm going to work here," Jed said. His voice sounded ridiculous in the silence. "Which bunk can I have?"

"Shet my tater trap," a man grinned. "Was wondering what it is. It is an ol' Billy Yank, sure 'nough. Last time I heard a voice like that, it was hollering, 'Retreat! Retreat!' "

"Maybe we oughta dig a barbecue pit and show him a Tehhexas welcome," drawled another.

"Naw. Looks sort o' scrawny. Afraid he'll only bile out to soup."

"Hawg soup, most like. I do smell a hawg most pure and plain."

The comments didn't sound particularly ribald, but not particularly menacing either. It was kind of a testing edge, Jed thought. He grinned uncertainly and walked down the middle of the room, looking for an unused bunk. As he did, the mouth organist struck up *Marching Through Georgia,* which drew a few grunts of laughter.

All the bottom bunks were in use, but he saw two adjoining empty top bunks. He could store his belongings on one. He heaved his saddlebags onto it.

"That's mine, boy. I put my stuff up there."

A man had gotten to his feet and was moving toward Jed. His squat, powerful body was so heavy, he rolled like a sailor on his short thick legs. He was shirtless, his blocky torso straining the seams of his dirty underwear. His blunt-jawed bullet head was bald as an egg and sank neckless into his massive shoulders. Jed had never seen such a man. He was pure brute.

"But there was nothing up there," Jed managed to say.

"I got it reserved."

The man's hairy arm reached past him, grabbed the saddle-bags and dumped them to the floor. Jed turned enough to face him, but the squat man only watched him with greenish unblinking eyes, his long arms hanging. He seemed to be waiting. Jed bent and picked up the saddlebags.

"I'll take the other one," he said.

"Naw. That's reserved too."

One man gave a whickering laugh, but nobody else did. Not stirring from his bunk,

Leandro Mirabel said: "Lea' the boy alone, Bull Jack, you big som bitch. He ain' half the size o' you."

"Tough," the squat man said.

Jed felt a sour twist in his belly. "Which of these bunks isn't reserved?"

"All reserved," Bull Jack said unblinkingly. "All of 'em."

Jed looked at him bewilderedly. "I don't understand. Do you just want to fight? If you do, why all this?"

Somebody laughed. "He just wants you to throw the first punch, sonny boy. Go ahead."

Bull Jack didn't move a muscle. He held his unsmiling stare on Jed.

The utter foolishness of it struck Jed. He couldn't just stand here and do nothing. Anyway it seemed like a big bluff. He turned, deliberately tossed his saddlebags onto the same bunk as before, then grabbed a post to swing himself up to the other vacant one. Immediately Bull Jack's thick fingers closed on the back of his belt and yanked. A moment later Jed was flat on the floor on his back, and then the saddlebags landed on his chest.

This time several men laughed.

Jed looked up at Bull Jack's gorilla form,

spraddle-legged beside him. He was still waiting. "My God," Jed heard himself say, "this is completely pointless."

And as he said it he felt his arms pushing him up to a crouch, his legs tightening under him, his body lifting and straightening fully, then his hand with the heavy saddlebags sweeping in a violent arc. Bull Jack threw up an arm, but the sudden swing caught him off guard. The loaded bags slammed him alongside the head and actually staggered him. But that was all.

Bull Jack growled and waded in. He aimed a clubbing blow that Jed only partly managed to duck. It caught him between his skull and hunched shoulder, squarely on the ear. Jed swung in the blaze of pain, clipping a hard left against Bull Jack's chin. The squat man fell back a step. Jed was a head taller than him and no weakling in spite of his gangling build. That seemed to surprise the cowhand.

Still he couldn't stand up long to this walking lump of muscle, Jed knew. He hadn't roughed-and-tumbled since he was a kid, while Bull Jack had the look of a seasoned barroom fighter, scars and all. The most Jed hoped for was to get in a few hurting licks before he was plowed down. The blazing sting of his ear seemed to clear his brain.

They circled and sparred for a few seconds. Jed found he was somewhat quicker and he drubbed Bull Jack lightly around the head and shoulders. He could have hit harder, but it would mean stepping inside range of those big arms.

And suddenly he was. Shifting patiently around, the squat man maneuvered him into a corner of the room. Rushing in, he caught Jed around the chest in a crushing hug, then swung him off his feet and hurled him against a bunk frame.

Jed was half-stunned by the impact. He grabbed at a bunkpost to hold himself upright, shaking his head to clear it. Bull Jack was already closing in on him, and Jed threw a quick right at his head. His knuckles bounced harmlessly off the round bullet skull and for an agonized instant Jed thought he'd cracked them.

Bull Jack caught him with a solid cuff across the head, knocking him away from the bunk. Still dazed, Jed tried to evade a follow-up blow. Bull lack's swing only tagged his shoulder, but it was enough to knock him backpedaling into the stove. It went over with a crash, Jed falling with it. A cloud of soot mushroomed across the clean-scrubbed floor and then the stovepipes came clanging down.

Groggy and helpless on his back, Jed saw Bull Jack loom above him, his boot lifted and poised, preparing to smash down on his face. Then a shot. Its racketing blast slammed like thunder between the walls. A flying particle of something stung Jed's face. He squeezed his eyes shut and then opened them.

Bull Jack was still standing above him, foot raised. He looked stupid with surprise. Then Jed saw that most of the heel of his boot had been ripped away. Leandro Mirabel, still on his bunk, was propped up on one elbow, grinning. His other hand held a smoking pistol.

"Ho boy," he said. "Ain' that a som bitch, though. The fight, I think she is end', eh?"

"You slipping sure as hell, Leandro," a crewman drawled. "You clean missed his foot."

"I know it. Som bitch! I mean to shoot the goddom thing clean off."

Chapter 4

Elizabeth followed Jed Starbuck with her eyes as he crossed the dark yard to the bunkhouse. But she wasn't particularly thinking about him, or about Aaron Troop towering beside her, talking soft-voiced, the touch of his hand respectful on her arm, his spurs ringing lightly on the patio flagstones as they walked. The night was warm on her face, yet she vaguely shivered and drew the worn *rebozo* tighter around her shoulders.

"I ran into this commission man at the roadhouse," Troop was saying, "and he says a fellow named McCoy has started a town at an old stage stop on the Butterfield line about fifty miles southwest of Kansas City. Has a deal with the railroad. Promised them he'll ship a million cattle over their line first season. Promises cattlemen a fair shake, cash on delivery and no fever quarantine."

"That sounds exciting," Eliitabeth said, but irony was always lost on Aaron. "What railroad?"

"The Kansas Pacific. They're building west to Denver and that means new railhead markets for Texas steers."

"Fine, if it's not just talk."

"Oh, this commission fellow saw the place. Says the rails been run through and there's shipping pens already built. Town is building up fast too. Abilene, they call it."

"I imagine Father is happy with the news."

"What Texas cowman wouldn't be?" Troop's tone was jubilant. "New Orleans was our big market before the war, but the trade has swung north. You know how much trouble we ran into last year with that herd I took up to Baxter Springs. Lost about a third of the cattle to raids and stampedes. Indians and Jayhawkers in the Strip. And all the Kansas sodgrubbers up in arms, claiming we were spreading tick and fever to their stock . . ."

"Let's sit down, shall we?"

'They moved toward a *ramada*-roofed bench that centered the patio. Why did I say I want to sit down? she wondered. I'm really too restless to sit. But she knew why. It had been something to say, anything that would fill the gaps in what passed for conversation with Aaron. No, she thought, that's not fair. Aaron was quite a man in his own way; he had an engaging strength and handled men well. He was surely no fool; not his fault he'd hardly scratched the rudiments of education.

They sat on the bench.

"Beth, I want to say something," Aaron began, his voice so serious that she thought no, not now please. But he didn't get it said. A clattering racket from the bunkhouse cut off his words. "What the devil's that?" he growled. "Suppose I'd better go see."

He stood up and Elizabeth said, "Good night, Aaron." He gazed at her a moment, his jaw hardening against the implied dismissal. He looked ready to say more, but then a gun was fired off in the bunkhouse. "Jesus!" he muttered. "Now what?"

He headed for the bunkhouse with loping strides, flung open the door and barged in. "What the hell is going on in here!" Elizabeth heard him roar. A burst of laughter from the crew. Just horseplay, probably directed against Jed Starbuck, the newcomer.

This made her think of her patient. It was time she checked on him again. The thought gave her a twinge of reluctance that she couldn't quite define.

All she knew was that Perry Starbuck made her uncomfortable. She'd never met a man like him. Such men as she'd known fitted into definitive types, good or bad. Different categories, but all recognizable. So she was sure of just one thing about Perry Starbuck. He defied category . . .

She entered the kitchen and said good night to Ceferina, who was washing dishes and cleaning up, refusing any help. Elizabeth passed through the house to the *sala* where her father was seated on the horsehair sofa, reading. He looked up at her, closed his book and lifted the steel-ringed spectacles off his nose.

"What's the shooting about?"

"Oh, the boys were cutting up a bit. Nothing serious."

The Major watched her a long, searching moment, then shook his head. "In this light—you know—"

"Yes, indeed. I look like Mother."

"Look, move, and talk like her." He sighed, rubbing a hand over his face. "Damn. Is this how a man grows old? Seems to get harder to hold onto what is." He looked at her. "Or maybe that's the trouble. A man tries too damned hard."

Elizabeth walked over to the sofa, bent and kissed him. "Now what does that mean?"

"You're young, Beth. A young marriage-able woman with her life ahead."

She laughed. "By most standards, I'm an old maid."

"I mean that too. It's no laughing matter, sis. You belong in the world. There are a passel of different places you could be and belong. One of 'em isn't a backwoods ranch a couple hundred miles from nowhere."

"I've been to those places, Father. This is my home."

"You belong in a home of your own. Not one I made for another woman. We had our life together, your mother and I. We lived and loved and raised three children. She's gone now, so are Chad and Paul. And you're a grown woman, ready for a life of your own. One that includes a husband, children . . ."

"Shouldn't that be my choice?"

He shook his head. "You've never had a choice. It was trained out of you. Those years at your Aunt Rachel's house in Baltimore. At school in Richmond. You'll never meet a man that's right for you in this country. Cowhands. Teamsters. Roughneck ranchers. Good men, many of 'em. But not a one that's suitable. That would suit you for a lifetime." He paused. "I doubt it'll ever get anywhere with you and Aaron. Be honest now—will it?"

"No, Father. But it's not really important."

"It is. Will be. You'll realize that one day." Lamplight polished his craggy face, limning it with tired shadow. "I won't be around forever. But that's not it. I might live a long time. Meantime you'd sour in this kind of life. Might be different if you were some pallid timid little thing. You're not. You're a strong vital woman, the kind that needs to live, really live, or go juiceless and hard, like a dried-up lemon. I don't aim to let that happen." He took her hands in his. "Before the year is out, I'm sending you down to Brownsville. You'll take a steamer East. I'll write Rachel; she'll be happy to have you with her again. You'll meet other young people. Men . . ."

"Suitable men," Elizabeth said quietly. "If you say so, Father."

"Damn it, sis, don't take on that martyred tone! You want to stay on and take care of the old man. Think I wouldn't like you to? Think this is easy for me? Seems a man's most comfortable habits get to be his deepest vices. I've been meaning to say this for a long time. You'll need a spell to think . . . adjust your mind to what's got to be."

"I'll certainly sleep on it. Here's to pleasant dreams." She forced a smile. "Are you going to bed soon?"

"Soon as I've finished with Marcus Aurelius. His *Meditations*. He was a wise old mossyhorn too. Better look in on our patient before your retire."

"I will. Father, what do you think of him . . . Perry Starbuck?" She didn't know why she asked; the words just came out.

"As you said—a strange one. Plenty of headstrong spunk. Damned pity if it got him killed before he learned to harness it to a constructive use. I'd say he and his brother are still finding themselves . . . they don't seem to have much else in common. Odd, that. Perry acts younger than his years, Jed older than his."

"Yet Perry is the leader—no question."

"H'mm. It might be a question of time only. Perry's a strong character, but I have a feeling his brother's not compliant— merely young."

"Perhaps. Good night, Father."

Elizabeth went to her room. She lighted the lamp on her commode, looking around at the adobe-walled room and simple furnishings which represented all that she called home. She was content here, she thought with a stab of bitter resentment. Her father thought she was strong, everyone did. But the roots of whatever strength she had were here, among the things she'd known since childhood. The knowledge that she might have to leave them forever came as a rude shock. Not altogether unexpectedly. Little things her father had said, other things he'd left unsaid, had half-prepared her.

She would, of course, do as she was told. She was an obedient daughter, had always been. Intelligent, sensitive, perceptive, she had opinions of her own. Characteristics that a woman generally had to suppress in favor of the man dominant in her life. First her father, later her husband. But Elizabeth had no serious thoughts of marriage; it had always been easy to place all affection in a father who seemed to personify the perfect man: wise, kind, strong yet tolerant, a leader of other men. None of the men she'd known in the East had ever quite measured up. Here, there was only Aaron Troop. Reliable, steady, dull Aaron. The rest of her father's crew were the kind of men she'd known all her life, simple, hard-working, abashed and humble in the presence of "good" women.

She understood and liked such men, and knew that she'd never be happy wedded to one of them.

Perhaps her father was right. You know he is, she thought, and gave a tight little shake of her head. Don't think about it. It doesn't help. If he says you must leave, you must, but don't think about it till you have to.

Leaving her room, she went down a short hallway, opened the door of Perry Starbuck's room and quietly entered. She turned up the low flame of the commode lamp, then crossed to the bed. He was lying quietly, eyes shut. She'd smoothed his blankets and was turning away when his eyes opened.

"Hello," he said.

"Hello. Did I wake you?"

"No."

He didn't smile. Didn't have to. His bright mocking eyes did it for him. He had no shame at all, it seemed. He'd quickly accepted the fact of her seeing his manly form stripped to the buff while she and Ceferina were cleaning him up and patching his private wounds. Something she'd done so many times while nursing incapacitated soldiers that she could view the task, even the male body itself, almost impersonally. Except for an occasional twinge of amusement at men's outright or badly concealed discomfort. But Starbuck hadn't been embarrassed. He'd actually seemed to enjoy himself. Or had successfully given the impression he did. Not offensively. Not by any trace of facial expression. He'd merely quietly mocked her all the while with that bold blue-green stare.

Just as he was doing now.

"You'd better try to sleep some more."

" 'Sleep doth knit up.' But I'm slept out for the moment."

She turned toward the door again.

"Wait," he said. She looked at him. He folded his hands under his head and smiled. Really smiled. "I think you ought to sit up with me awhile. I'm a sick man."

"A sick man needs his sleep."

"Please. Can we talk a little?"

Elizabeth moved a hand-carved chair close to the bed, her petticoats making crisp intimate rustlings as she seated herself. She sat very still, hands folded primly, on her knees. "You might be interested to know that my father intends to offer you a job on his crew. He's already hired your brother."

"Is that right?" He watched her. Just

watched her with those bright cool eyes till she felt her nerves quiver.

"I'm sorry," she snapped. "I didn't mean to get you all excited."

"Don't be offended. Merely wondering why he'd take on a pair of unskilled Yankees. Charity?"

"Does it matter why? Do you accept or don't you?"

"We do. With thanks."

"You may thank my father. Do you always speak for your brother?"

Starbuck laughed, grimacing a little against the pull of stitches around his mouth.

"Is that so amusing?"

"Just that Parral fellow nearly took my scalp off and you seem bound to finish the job. To answer your question. Jed's eight years my junior and I've pretty much taken care of him all his life. Which isn't really any of your business, Miss Hobart. I'm grateful to you and your father and consider myself in your debt. My gratitude doesn't extend to baring my private life for your perusal. Is that clear?"

She felt her face grow hot. "Are you always so . . . outspoken?"

"Why not say rude?"

"I—I suppose I was the rude one. I'm sorry."

"Forget it."

He yawned, wincing a little as he stretched himself under the blankets. He was, she knew, big and hard and superbly knit, not an ounce of fat on him. She caught her thoughts up tightly, feeling a wave of embarrassment.

"What do you think of me, Miss Hobart?"

She wondered if he'd cultivated his way of putting things: suddenly, disconcertingly, tipping you off balance as if he were thinking a half step ahead of you. That's ridiculous, she thought. All right, if he wanted to spar. "What do you think I think, Mr. Starbuck?"

"I think you're fascinated."

She stood up and his hand moved and caught her wrist.

"Let go of me, please."

It was strange, the way his hand held her. Like iron, yet very gently, as if he knew his strength and could do with it exactly as he chose. Stranger the way she felt herself yield even as she pulled against the pressure of his drawing her to him, close, closer. Their faces were inches apart; their lips touched.

His hand opened, she pulled back and

straightened up. "Call it a tribute to beauty," he said.

She scrubbed the back of her hand across her mouth and said evenly, "If your face weren't full of stitches, I'd slap it. If you ever do that again, I will slap it."

"Will you?"

"Try it."

He laughed. An easy good-natured laugh. "I don't care to. You've had a long day. Why don't you go to bed?"

She stared at him a long moment. "You did that so easily," she whispered. "I don't . . ."

"Understand? Simple. I want to do a thing, I do it. Other men, the men you've known, would face a loaded shotgun before taking a minor liberty. Which is plain damn' stupid. How much courage did that take just now? The sky didn't fall, the ground didn't open and swallow me. I didn't think it would." His eyes danced with dry kindling lights. "Taboos. Rules. Proprieties. Dead bones. Touch 'em and they crumble. You've never met a man like me, that's all."

"I've never met such insufferable arrogance. I think my father was wrong in deciding to take you on. I think I'll tell him so."

"There you go. You should. If you're that afraid of me, do it."

"I'll do what I please and not on your say-so." She felt coldly furious. "I suppose when you're well, you'll go back on Parral land and draw more lightning."

"I'm going to live there. I told 'em that. What I say I'll do, I do."

"Why did you have to come here? Stir up trouble?"

"I didn't bring it. I only found it." A smile flicked the corner of his mouth. "It's fun. It's a living. I'm crazy. I'm the snake in Eden. Take your choice."

"I'd say all of them." She walked to the door and paused, hand on the latch. "Tell me something."

"Another personal question?"

"Yes. Is anything sacred to you? Do you believe in anything?"

"Myself."

"I knew you'd say that."

"But you had to hear it, didn't you?"

Elizabeth stepped out quickly, closed the door and went down the hall to her room. She latched the door behind her, then shot the bolt. Setting the lamp on the commode, she began to unfasten the throat of her dress. Stopped. Looked at her reflection in the scrollwork-framed mirror, her mouth a trembling stain in her white face.

She blew out the lamp and finished undressing in the dark.

She stood a moment in the silky blackness, her heart pounding, tingling with a sense of womanhood she'd never known. Slowly she ran her hands from her thighs and hips and belly up to her full breasts. Suddenly, fiercely, she pressed her fingers deep into the smooth warm globes. God, she thought, dear God, not him.

Chapter 5

Since saving him from Bull Jack's attentions, Leandro Mirabel seemed to have taken a special interest in Jed's welfare. "I'm show you all you got to know," Leandro told him. "Bot Jee-zos, you are soch a clomsy som bitch, she's going to take planty time. You got the farm moscles. Hah. You got to build diff'rent kind moscles to work the *brasada.*" He inspected Jed's clothes and equipment and shook his head. "Tha's no good; forst you need the *brasadero* outfit."

Brasadero clothes, Leandro explained, were designed to keep at least part of your hide on your body rather than lose it all to *brasada* thorn and cactus. First his cloth jacket with the skirted hem must go; it would snag, it would tear all to hell. Leandro loaned Jed his own spare jacket, a short leather one padded at the elbows to let you fend off the mesquite by throwing your bent arms out. An amiable puncher named Poke Tanner consented to loan Jed his extra chaps, a pair cut in the narrow Cheyenne style, to replace the open-range batwings which would hang up on brush. "Cot two inch from aroun' the brim of your sombrero," Leandro instructed Jed. "Make her narrow. The rawhide *barbequejo*, she mus' go. The chin snap mus' be so thin, she snap like string if hat cotch on brush, *sabe*?" He measured Jed's *riata*, then whipped out his knife and hacked off about twenty feet before Jed could even object. "You ain' rope no good in brosh with all this goddom clothesline."

Jed really balked at the worn but suitable cowman's boots that Leandro dug out of the storeroom gear. But Leandro argued so vehemently and persuasively that he finally gave in. Hanging onto farm shoes that weren't practical in this country was a piece of foolish sentiment. Leandro also provided

69

a pair of *vaquero*'s spurs; Poke suggested that Jed file the rowels blunt so as not to cut his horse up unnecessarily. Leandro remarked that only domb som bitch chicken-heart' Anglos worried about such things, then grinningly indicated his own blunt-filed rowels.

Leandro was a real character, Jed thought, but he was glad enough of his help. He was also somewhat ashamed of his earlier thoughts about Mexicans in general.

In the morning, the crew rode out to Tuley Spring and the gather pens. These were built of sizable scrub oak harvested from the chaparral, trimmed of branches and skidded down to the flats. The posts were sunk three feet into the earth and lashed together with strips of green cowhide, forming corrals that would hold the toughest and wildest longhorns. The job at hand was to haze all the branded stock they could find on TH's southeast range over to the pens. As they worked the mottes and thickets, they were also to pick up and brand calves that had missed branding in the spring.

Jed had believed he was a reasonably good rider. He'd always held a saddle fairly well; the buttsores and chafed thighs he'd picked up on the long ride from Austin had hardened out. But he soon realized how much he had to learn.

The cowhunters rode single file in groups of twos or threes, using small bunches of cattle for decoys as they worked through the tangles of chaparral and mesquite. Whenever they flushed out a longhorn, they'd break into a furious pursuit, the lead horse hitting the brush flat on and tearing out a hole of sorts for those behind. Bent low in their saddles, they hurdled bent mesquite trunks, ducked live-oak branches and switched across solid stretches of prickly pear. Their brush ponies cleared the bristling cacti like jackrabbits and plowed through ten-foot-high thorn thickets, slashing their chests and legs, sharing the reckless frenzy of their riders.

Jed kept up as well as he could, trying to take in everything at once. But he knew that he'd be weeks just learning basic skills and that he'd be of little use on a cowhunt till he did. He watched Rubio Perez charge after a liver-colored calf and whirl out his *riata*, snapping a figure-eight loop over its hind feet. It looked like an impossibly difficult throw. Rubio reined past Jed and Leandro, dragging the bawling calf toward a branding fire. He was a wiry runt of a man with a face like lined leather, his brown-stained teeth grinning around the *cigarita* clamped beween them. He winked at them. *"Un-ladino pure,"* he said. "A ver' bad one."

Jed said: "Could I ever learn to rope like that?"

"It is nothing," Leandro chuckled. "She's only tak' you seven year.

"Seven years!"

"Sure. She's tak' Rubio that long, starting when he's a kid. Is call' *colear*—underhanding the loop and hindfooting the cow. Is planty tricky thing. I can do her some, but nobody do her good as Rubio. Is forst thing you batter lorn, the *riata*. I show you."

For the rest of the morning, Leandro gave practical demonstrations on the large and fine points of casting a rope. How to keep the loop small because you couldn't cast a broad one in chaparral. How to get on top of a steer before throwing, going over the withers when possible, otherwise dabbing back of the horns with a honda to make a figure eight that would pick up the forehoofs as well as the neck. How to heel or *colear*, snagging an animal by the hind feet, the hardest throw of all but the quickest and most efficient one, if you could manage it, of catching up the brush-wise beeves of the *brasada.* Leandro kept urging Jed to throw a loop on this bush or that small tree, savagely cursing all his efforts. "No, no! Jee-zos, I never see soch a domb son of a cow! How many times I got to show you? Like *this,* see? *Hijo de puta,* you are all thombs . . ."

Jed kept doggedly at it, sweating away the hours, wondering why he wasn't getting anywhere and growing a healthy hatred for Leandro who handled his *riata* with a lightning wizardry that seemed to have been born into his arm. And suddenly, he couldn't have said exactly when or how, Jed felt a nudge of real dexterity in his arm, an increasing accurary in his throws. He didn't think Leandro noticed; the *vaquero* never slacked up his wicked berating of him.

As they threaded through the brush mottes, occasionally spooking up a longhorn, Leandro did all the real roping. Finally he let Jed try his luck with a rather docile and puny-looking calf. "There you go," Leandro waved a hand. "Tail him down and cotch him up."

Jed did his best, crashing through the massed chaparral in pursuit. When he finally cornered the calf, he missed two throws before dropping a loop over its bead. He didn't feel too exultant as he dragged the bawling animal toward a fire. But Leandro said casually, "Is hokay for forst cotcb. Now you practice more, hah? *Hola!*"

Leandro took after a mouse-colored cow, his pony skimming in powerful bounds across some low thickets. Jed stared after him. Then he moved on, smarting with a sense of inadequacy. He'd caught one and he'd catch more, by God. But Leandro made it look so damned easy.

Still Jed had to admit to a glimmer of excitement in this new life. It held a hard, passionate vigor such as he'd never experienced. Something even seemed communicated to him from the springy flow of muscles in the piebald mustang under him. Leandro was so dead serious about his role as tutor, that at the corrals this morning he'd refused to let the men fix Jed up with a gaunt wicked-eyed pinto which they averred was the gentlest boss in the outfit. "You crazy som bitches," Leandro had said. "You want to get this domb kid kill' his forst day?" He'd selected another horse for Jed, though it almost meant a fight with the wrangler who'd begun the joke. Almost. Nobody wanted to take on Leandro, including Bull Jack last night.

Ahead of Jed, a huge longhorn rose out

of the ground, or seemed to. A great speckled beast with a drooped horn. He crashed
away in a straight run through a heavy jag
of chaparral. Jed cut hard around the chaparral, hearing the bull wallowing through. It
sounded as if he were hung up in the brush.
Jed plowed into the thickets toward the
sound.

He broke suddenly into an open spot
where the bull was trying to batter his way
into deeper brush. Jed pulled up quickly as
the bull veered around at bay, his tail lashing.
Seeing him at close range, gaunt and muscled, his hide a mass of thorn scars, Jed realized for the first time what he'd tackled.
He tried to wheel the piebald, but too late.
The bull was already barreling toward them,
head lowered.

He crashed into them flank-on, catching
the piebald behind the girth and just missing
Jed's leg. Man and horse went down in a
kicking, sprawling tangle. The bull turned
and trotted away, then spun around and
charged again.

Abruptly Leandro was there, surging out
of the brush and lunging his pony toward
the bull at right angles. His reins were
wrapped around his left arm, his drawn gun
in his right hand. He let out a whoop as he

fired. The bullet whomped into the bull's heavily muscled shoulder, causing him to swerve off from his quarry. Switching targets, he went after Leandro, who cut sharply toward him, then angled past him at the last moment.

As he passed the bull, Leandro fired into his left horn close to the skull. The horntip raked along his pony's haunch and drew blood. Leandro pulled up and pivoted his mount around, but the bawling bull plunged on through the chaparral in full retreat.

"Hah!" Leandro grinned. "Is nothing like shoot' into quick of horn to knock fight from big mean *chongo.*"

He dropped to the ground and tramped over to Jed, who lay half-stunned where he'd fallen. His right leg had been briefly pinned by the downed piebald, who had rolled to his feet and now stood quivering. Leandro inspected the animal first. "Ho boy, is dom lucky that *chongo,* he got on'y one horn. The one horn, she's miss. The other horn, she's not there or I'm think she's rip the gots out of one fine horse."

He coldly eyed Jed as he climbed to his feet, rubbing his leg. He was vaguely surprised to find it uninjured. The soft earth must have saved it from being crushed or broken.

"So," Leandro said, nodding slowly, "he's got to prove himself even if he's get a good horse kill' for it, hah?" Jed must have looked as abashed as he felt, because Leandro added mildly: "Look, *vaquero*, don' push her so hard. There is time for all things in this world. You will lorn. Jos' tak' you time. Hah, bot maybe I should have tell you about soch *chongos* like that big mean ory-eye."

Jed nodded dazedly. "I guess so."

Leandro explained that the old *chongo* was the kind of outlaw who'd outwitted cowhunters so long that nothing short of a bullet could stop him. One of the tricky old mossyhorns who'd learned to lie low in brush and who, even when caught in a gather, sometimes wormed their way free by crawling out through the tightest thickets on their knees. Eluding capture for many years gave those old *bastardos* so fierce a taste for freedom that they'd charge a would-be captor on horseback as quickly as a man on foot. Cornered, it took several riders to rope and subdue them; then they'd like as not "sull" themselves to death, as the Anglo riders called it. Dragged away toward the pens and captivity, they would suddenly collapse, shudder, and die.

"This," Leandro concluded with a kind of romantic flourish, "we *vaqueros* call *acolambrao*. Is not som'thing an Anglo can com'prend. Bot I think maybe you call it a broken heart."

Days went by. Jed threw himself doggedly into the work. His riding improved; he learned to throw a passable *riata*. He soon learned that Leandro had been right. A man needed to develop his muscles all over again in this kind of work. Some mornings he'd wake feeling like one mass of aches and twinges. He had to force himself to move and he felt tired nearly all the time. Thanks to his youth, though, these effects vanished quickly. At first he lost more weight than his already gangling frame could spare, wasting down to skin and bone, but soon began to put it back on in slabs of lean muscle. Within two weeks, he noticed the difference.

Of course the crew had a lot of fun at his expense, but he'd worked before with crews of men, at harvests and barn-raisings and the like. The newcomer and youngest man could always expect a rough hazing. Jed took it good naturedly and worked hard, willing to pull his weight and then some; the verbal and practical jokes began to slacken off. Leandro summed it up. "You are liked," he said.

But there was one exception, and that was Bull Jack. Jed made a few tentative friendly gestures toward him, but quickly found that the bald, surly, thickset man wasn't having any. It bothered Jed till he realized that Bull Jack had no friends and didn't want any. Men like him could be found everywhere, Leandro quietly pointed out; most of the time they minded their own business and asked only to be left alone. They were to be neither hated not pitied; if the good God were satisfied with what he had made, why should men question?

One evening, as the crew rode into headquarters in a dusty bunch, Perry and Miss Elizabeth were sitting on the bench inside the walled patio. The crew passed close by the patio, and Jed felt a momentary pleasure in seeing Perry up and around. The wound in his leg had confined him to bed these two weeks and, though it contradicted his usual restless energy, he hadn't seemed to mind much. Jed had visited his room every night and Perry had spoken of getting back on his feet soon.

A cane lay on the flagstones beside the bench. Elizabeth had a book open on her lap and was reading to him. A pleasing picture, Jed thought, till he saw Perry lean toward her and say something. Elizabeth jerked away from him, snapped the book shut, stood up and walked into the house, her chin high.

Perry picked up his cane and got to his feet, grinning a little. He waved a hand at Jed, who didn't wave back. Before this, he'd seen Perry play callous games with women, and he'd never liked it.

Looking away from him, Jed surprised the look on Aaron Troop's hard-knobbed face. It was almost a blank look. Yet the color had left his weathered skin. Jed wasn't surprised at Troop's jealousy of Perry, only how deeply it seemed to go. If Aaron hadn't been getting anywhere with Elizabeth before, at least he'd had no rival. Perry, bound to a sickbed, had all the advantage.

But Troop couldn't be sure that anything had developed between Elizabeth and him. Even Jed wasn't sure, and knowing Perry, he'd been watchful. He hadn't often been present when Perry and Elizabeth were together, but when he was, he'd been conscious of a nervous constraint in her: it clashed with her usual poise, and Perry must be the cause.

After supper in the cookshack, Jed went to the house to look in on Perry in his room. He was bright-eyed and cheerful; his face still wore some livid scars that would be a long time healing. He figured he'd be ready to go to work for Major Hobart in another week or so.

Jed decided the time had come to have it out once and for all about the Mora River land. Perry had made no reference to it since they had come to the TH.

"I've been thinking some more about your notion to build on the Mora."

"Have you?"

"You go ahead if you want," Jed said flatly. "But if you do, I want my share of the money. I'll just pull out of it."

Perry gave him a sharp look. "Seems you've grown a few hard edges on your head as well as your shoulders." He grinned. "Let's cross that bridge when we come to it. Maybe I'll change my plans. Let's stick on here awhile . . ."

Jed eyed him bleakly. "Do I have to remind you that Miss Elizabeth is a *real* lady?"

"Bless your bones, boy, who said she's not?"

"Well, the way I saw you when we came in—"

"Having a little fun was all. Man gets restless lying and sitting around with nothing to do. She's the princess of the castle. Out of my class."

Jed wasn't sure whether to believe him or not. "Did you notice how Aaron Troop looked at you? He's crazy jealous."

"I'd say that's Troop's problem."

"Unless he makes it your problem."

Perry laughed. "Sour apples, fella. You've never had much luck with girls and you don't much like seeing me have any . . ."

You couldn't score points debating with Perry. Jed gave it up. Yet—just why would Perry change his plans?

When he left the house, Elizabeth and Aaron Troop were in the patio. Jed could barely see them in the thickening dusk, but he plainly heard their voices as he stepped out the door. He halted there, embarrassed.

"Never assume that you have any claim on me, Aaron," Elizabeth was saying in a brittle voice. "You haven't."

"No," Troop said softly, bitterly. "I reckon not. But I'm free to offer any opinion I want. And I am warning you against this fellow Starbuck."

"Indeed?"

"God, Beth! Can't you see through the man? He's a damn' opportunist if I ever seen one. Way he's laid around mooching off you Hobarts . . ."

"With a bad leg wound, do you expect him to stand around? Be fair, Aaron. This isn't like you."

"I seen his kind before," Troop said doggedly. "I can smell a shorthorn like him a mile off. You hear me now, Beth. For your own good, get rid of him. Tell your pa to. Or there'll come a time you'll be sick whenever you think of the day you took him in."

"Not as sick as I feel right now. Not by half, Aaron—"

Troop swung on his heel and tramped away, his spurs ringing savagely on the stones till he passed out the gate. Elizabeth stood briefly as she was, her lawn dress a pale blur in the night. She turned and started for the door, coming into the soft spill of windowlight. Her head was bent, she was fingering a rose she held. Becoming aware of Jed, she stopped.

"Didn't mean to listen," he said embarrassedly.

"I'm sure you didn't." It might have been light irony, but she did smile. "Isn't this a sorry excuse for a rose? Prairie Queen roses . . . my mother planted the bushes years ago and they never did take well." Her eyes were fixed on his as she talked, and Jed's face grew warm. "Why don't we sit down, Mr. Starbuck? Something I want to ask you."

Jed waited for her to seat herself on the *ramada* bench, then eased uncomfortably down beside her. "I can come right to the point, I suppose." She brushed the rose lightly over her lips. "I'd like to hear all that you can tell me about your brother."

He'd guessed as much; Perry was pretty close-mouthed about himself. "Uh—that's a tall order . . ."

"Well, whatever comes to mind. You told us some that first night."

So Jed filled in the gaps for her. He didn't soften the hard facts that, ordinarily, he'd never elaborate on to anyone outside his family. He didn't want her to keep any illusions about Perry. Their father had built from scratch the biggest farm in their Ohio county, he told her, and Perry had always been the apple of Pa's eye. The two had been a lot alike, full of ideas how to grow bigger and better. Pa had sent Perry to school to learn about newfangled methods of farming, but the war had broken off his education. Shortly after Perry had enlisted in the cavalry, their mother had died.

She'd always provided a rein on Pa's grandiose ambitions, keeping him from batting off on one crazy junket or another. After her death, he'd gone sort of haywire, drinking heavily, investing in various harebrained schemes. When Perry had returned from the war to find Pa dead and the farm deep in debts, he and Jed had tried to put the place back on a paying basis. But it was far too big for two men to handle and they couldn't afford to pay out wages. Perry had flatly refused to sell off part of the land in order to acquire working capital. That was never his way; he wanted the whole hog or nothing, a tendency inherited from Pa. But he had Ma's iron will, and once he'd gotten the notion of stalking out a large piece of Texas, hail and rain and lightning couldn't change him.

When Jed had finished, Elizabeth sat silent, gently tapping her foot. Her light perfume was heavy and disturbing in the near-dark. She gave a soft, strange laugh. "Well, you can guess. I'm fascinated by him. And repelled too. I suppose that sounds strange . . . or merely feminine."

"I don't know."

"You don't, do you? You're not much like him."

"Miss Beth." His words formed even as the thought did: warn her straight out. "There are a lot of things about my brother that possibly you don't understand. But there's one thing you can be sure of. Back of it all, he's ambitious." He paused lamely. "I thought you should know."

She gave him a quick, odd look. "Oh? What made you think I don't?"

Chapter 6

A week to the day later, Perry was up and around, still limping a little but no longer needing a cane. On that day he reported for work, and the boys crowded the "opera house" —the top rail of the corral fence—to watch him fork his first cowpony. They'd considerately roped and saddled one for him, and Poke Tanner led it out. "You been a sick man," Poke drawled. "Better start off on something gentle."

Jed stared. It was the same ugly-eyed pinto that Leandro had prevented them from mounting him on. He stepped close to Perry as he took the rein, saying in an urgent mutter, "If you don't want that leg to split open again, get another!"

Perry grinned. "A real woollywhyhow, eh? Figured as much."

Abruptly he seized the cheek strap above the bit and yanked the pony's head around till it almost touched the saddle. By now Jed knew that this was called "cheeking"; any rider did it with an unknown horse, but he was surprised that Perry knew the trick. Then he remembered, his brother's four years with the U. S. Cavalry.

With the pinto unable to ruckus till he'd swung into the saddle, Perry merely gave him a touch of the rein to halt his prancing. "He's gentle right enough. I do appreciate this, fellows . . ."

Perry plunged into the work with tremendous zest. Jed himself was proving out about as well as a greenhorn might expect to after a few weeks on the job. But Perry's progress was amazing. The cavalry years had merely honed fine an instinctive feel he had with horseflesh. He was soon turning a peg pony on a biscuit without cutting the crust, a handy talent for working brush country where a man who could twist and turn a running horse through the worst of it had the best chance of keeping his hide on.

Perry had a natural facility with the *riata* too; after only a week, practicing with the lariat at odd times, he was going into the fine points of roping that Leandro had shown Jed. Rubio Perez, best roper on the crew, said that he'd never before seen a *Yanqui* who was such a natural *hechichero de cuero*—a wizard of the leather. While Major Hobart vowed that the last man he'seen ride like Perry had been a Comanche who'd sent ten arrows into a target inside of a minute at full gallop, the target having been a dead horse the Major was lying behind.

It surprised everyone except Jed, who was used to it. Perry had always done everything too damned easily and too damned well. His prowess didn't stop with riding and roping. In a few days he'd eased past the crew's reservations about Yankees and greenhorns, winning them over with that wry, engaging way he had that drew people in spite of themselves. It had been far easier for him than for Jed, and Jed didn't deny that it irked him. But then it always had—the way Perry won so easily and completely what others were lucky they could partly master and then only by hard work and patience.

The cowhunt continued, a hard bitter grind that filled Jed's days from dawn to dark till it began to seem as if he'd been on this job all his life, that any existence he'd known before it was shadowy and unreal.

The work went well. When Aaron Troop could report to Hobart that they had nearly five thousand head in the hunt pens, the Major announced his satisfaction. They'd split the gather into two herds and start the drives next week. Tomorrow Troop would go up to Moratown and see about hiring extra men to fill out the drive crews. One herd, trailbossed by Troop, would point north toward the new railhead at Abilene. Rubio Perez would boss the other drive to the usual destination of New Orleans, always a sure market but not a very profitable one. A Kansas drive contained several elements of risk. But putting what he knew about the beef-hungry Eastern markets to which the Kansas Pacific Railroad would connect together with what he'd learned about Joseph McCoy's new town, Hobart judged it worth the gamble.

Jed half-listened to the Major discussing it with his range boss. The two Starbucks, along with Leandro Mirabel and Poke Tanner, had just hazed a bunch of cows into one of the empty pens. Leandro swung down to lift the gate poles into place and thong them down. The others dismounted and led their horses to the muddy edge of the spring. The Major was on the high seat of a buckboard in which he'd driven here; a recurrent arthritis held him almost exclusively to this way of getting about.

"This Abilene thing has its drawbacks, Major," Troop cautioned, leaning an arm on the wagon box. "Long ways to Kansas. Lots of cow-lifting Choctaws in the Nations. And jayhawker gangs who'll hit anything on the hoof. We could lose a lot of head. And I ain't so sure we can swing around that Kansas fever quarantine . . ."

Hobart motioned brusquely with his pipe. "That commission fellow thought we can. Said we can follow Jesse Chisholm's old trade road north of Belton. A Kansas market could mean bonanza. If it does fall flat, it surely won't bust us. We'll chance it, Aaron."

Jed, watering his horse, didn't pay them too much attention because he was surreptitiously watching the two young women sitting their sidesaddled mounts beside a fence, talking in the animated way girls did when they seldom saw one another and had lots of catching up to do. They'd ridden out here with the Major. Elizabeth looked predictably smart in a green corduroy riding habit and wide-brimmed straw hat. She'd added a veil, but her chin and throat which the hatbrim didn't shade was starting to pinken just the same.

Mainly, though, Jed sneaked glances at her companion. So did Poke and two other young punchers over by the pens. Even if this weren't a near-womanless country, Elizabeth's friend would get second looks. She wasn't beautiful in Beth Hobart's classic way; she wasn't even pretty, strictly speaking. But she had a pert elfin face that took your glance right away. It was lively and vivacious, with small boyish features and bright tar spot eyes that seemed to take in everything at once. She was black-haired, but her skin was almost as white as Elizabeth's, though it took the sun a lot better; her throat was lightly tanned. She was slender, almost little, and if she had a figure, it was lost in the bulky riding costume she wore. It seemed to have been tailored for a bigger sister, and she didn't look more than eighteen, maybe only seventeen.

The men mounted again and started past the pens. They rode close by the girls and

Perry pulled up, touching his hat and showing his teeth. "Good morning, Miss Hobart!"

Elizabeth nodded coolly. "Good morning. We haven't seen much of you since you moved to the bunkhouse."

"Your gain—my loss."

She compressed her lips. "Would you and your brother wait a moment, please?"

Without waiting for a reply, she nudged her mount over to her father's buckboard. Leandro gave Poke a comical browlifted glance, and the two headed away into the chaparral. Elizabeth spoke to her father and Jed heard Aaron Troop say something about "bad example." He sounded angry. The Major said something and nodded, and Elizabeth cantered her horse back to them, her color a little high.

"Father says we can ride back in the chaparral if the brothers Starbuck accompany us. Gentlemen, this is my friend, Elena Parral. These are Jed and Perry Starbuck."

"I'm afraid the name is familiar," the smaller girl said. "Which of you did my brother whip?"

"Me," Perry grinned, snapping off his hat. The sun blazed on his tawny hair. *"Lo siento muchismo,* Señorita Parral!"

"Why? It's I who should be sorry, señor."

"No, I. That we couldn't meet under more likely circumstances."

"Come along," Elizabeth said sharply. "Are we going to ride or not?"

"Be careful," Troop called after them, a harsh strain in his voice. "You men watch out for the ladies, hear? Ride slow and keep to the open places like the Major said. There's some mean mossyhorns in that brush . . ."

"What a bore," Elizabeth murmured, flicking her boot with her riding crop. "Anyone for a race?"

Perry laughed quietly. "Better do as you're told. We'll ride as far as Kenobee Creek and back."

"Will we? Are you giving the orders?"

They threaded across the stony ground between heavy clots of *brasada* brush, Perry and Elizabeth riding ahead of Jed and Elena. Once they disturbed a pair of road runners who went whizzing away in gray blurs. Jed felt uncomfortable beside Elena Parral. He didn't know what to say to her . . . particularly with bad blood between their brothers. Elena looked serene and untroubled, her lively face rather controlled, and she didn't say anything either.

They came on some TH *vaqueros* trailing a bunch of wild ones toward the pens. The Mexicans had developed a method of cowhunting for which Americans lacked the patience and feel. Pushing some placid decoy cattle in front of them, they'd close in gradually on the wild stock, singing a wordless, coaxing, rhythmic song that swelled to quivering heights or ebbed to a soothing, sobbing beat. After an hour or more, continuing the soporific lullaby, they'd have the decoys pretty well merged with the wild ones. Then they'd press the lot of them slowly in the direction of the pens. It was a tricky business. The riders had to keep their distance on light-stepping horses. Anything, a shuffled hoof, a rattled bit chain, could spook the cattle. But they had this bunch under control, crowding them tighter and faster as they neared the pens.

"Isn't it marvelous, how they do that?" Elizabeth asked. "I never tire of watching it."

"Very pretty," Perry said dryly. "Rope as many and drag 'em in, they could do the same in half the time."

"I'm glad you're such an expert after two weeks," Elizabeth said in a gibing tone. She pulled up her horse and looked at the other girl. " 'Lena, suppose that you ride ahead with Mr. Jed Starbuck. Don't wait for us."

A puckish humor touched Elena Parral's lips. "I hope we don't get lost. Or that you don't. Shall we ride fast or slowly, Beth?"

"However you like."

Elizabeth's tone was tart. Jed met Perry's amused glance, then fell in beside Elena as they moved on toward the creek. The stiff heavy folds of her draped riding skirt seemed to hamper Elena; she kept giving it little irritable flounces with one gloved hand. A tomboyish gesture that (he thought) more or less expressed boredom. Jed didn't blame her, but he couldn't help thinking: I'll bet if she could ride like a man, she would ride like hell. The idea made him uncomfortable; only female circus riders and the like rode that way. He'd heard that Spanish ladies were even more constricted by proprieties than Anglo ladies, and therefore it seemed strange that Elena's family permitted her to ride alone and unchaperoned, especially when calling on Anglos.

"Would you like something to eat?" she asked languidly. "I brought along some bread and cheese."

"No—thanks." He felt unaccountably irritated. "I suppose Miss Beth arranged to bring you out here today."

"So that we could all ride out of Major Hobart's sight and she could be alone with your brother?" Elena nodded thoughtfully. "Partly true, I suppose. It was mere chance that I called on the Hobarts today and that the Major decided to ride out to the pens. But Beth was suddenly anxious that we both accompany him. She didn't tell me anything, but it's obvious. I'm along to divert you." Her tone was amused. "Are you and your brother always together?"

"It's a family custom. And I suppose this is a rare outing for you. I mean, don't your people keep a pretty tight rein on their women?"

She made a face at him. "All the time. Actually my father is rather liberal as elderly dons go. My mother was an Anglo, you see. A Boston girl, daughter of an Army officer. They met in San Francisco shortly after your Captain Frémont seized Sonoma in 1846. And I was sent to Boston for my education."

She said it sort of archly, which prompted Jed to say: "I've *taught* school, myself."

"Oh?" She showed a shade more respect. "Where was this?"

"Ohio." A kind of abashed honesty made him add: "It was just a one-room country school."

"But that is a fine calling—to teach the young."

He was glad she didn't press for details. Riding slowly, chatting a little as they rode, feeling more at ease with one another, they reached the west bank of the Kenobee. The creek was a sallow twist of water that angled across TH's southeast range and lost itself in the Mora.

"I hope," Elena said carefully, "that your brother has given up his idea of settling by the Mora River."

"So do I."

"You're not sure?"

"That's about it."

"What my brother did to him was terrible. But it will be worse if he comes back." She slanted a veiled look at Jed. "What will you do then?"

"I won't be with him," Jed said flatly. "I've told him that."

"I'm glad."

Downstream above the bank, a TH hand had just dragged a roped calf over to a branding fire and another puncher was tying it. They watched as he took an iron from the fire, holding it in both gloved hands as he slapped it on the cow's flank.

"This *brasada*," Elena murmured. "It's a strange, cruel place, is it not?"

"I don't know," Jed said. "At first I couldn't see doing that to animals. But it seems to be necessary."

"I was not really thinking of the animals. I was thinking of what men in this land do to each other." She gave him a fragment of a smile. "Shall we turn back? Perhaps Beth and your brother have finished their conversation."

"So you've had a change of heart," Perry Starbuck said mildly.

"What do you mean?" Elizabeth asked, though she knew well enough.

"You've been avoiding me for two weeks."

She saw the familiar mockery and challenge in his gaze The two of them were standing, dismounted, behind a pale green-shield of mesquite, holding their reins. Standing a few feet apart, they had almost the stance of antagoists. Irritably Elizabeth slapped her riding crop against her skirt.

"You're not our guest now. You work for my father, I'm his daughter. We can't just cross that line whenever we like."

"Huh-uh. That's not it. If you won't cross the line, just say the word and I will. You know that." He smiled boyishly. "You keep fighting what you feel. *That's* it."

She felt a rush of blood around her heart. "What do I feel? Tell me—"

"You're a delicately bored lady who's piqued by curiosity about me. What you keep telling yourself, isn't it?"

"Do I?"

"To give yourself the necessary excuse for what's obvious: you came to see me. Even brought along a friend to take care of my little brother."

"He's nearly as big as you, or haven't you ever noticed?"

He grinned. "It's my experience that someone who answers a question with another question is dodging the truth."

Elizabeth colored. Why couldn't he be sly or devious? Then it would be easy to detest him. Instead he slashed to the heart of things with an unsparing honesty. "Are you so sure I am?"

"There you go again. Question for a question. I guess it's time we found out."

He moved toward her. She gripped the riding crop tightly:"Do you really care to try?"

"'That's right. You're supposed to hit me this time."

She stared at him. His hands reached out and swayed her to him. Her whole body felt loose and heavy, yet taut with expectancy. Her lips parted.

"Do you want to hit me?"

"No," she whispered. "I want you to kiss me. Please kiss me."

She did not know how long it lasted. Finally she drew back a little, hands flat against his chest, her face lowered. "I think you have proven what you wanted to."

He raised her chin. "Look at me. There. You think I'm playing a game with you? I'm not."

"If you're not, then" —again she felt a flaring heat in her face— "you'll ask Father's consent. Ask him today."

He showed a small crooked smile. "He won't give it."

"Why won't he?"

"He doesn't like me."

"Oh, Perry, that's ridiculous! Why shouldn't he like you?"

"One evening when you'd retired early, we played chess," he said enigmatically. "After that . . ." He shrugged. "You'd better ask him."

"I shall." She closed her eyes and lifted her face. "Oh, I love you," she whispered fiercely. "I don't care, I don't care! I love you . . ."

In a few minutes Jed Starbuck and Elena came back, riding slowly. Holding Perry's hand, Elizabeth faced them both and said: "We're going to be married." She was aware that her voice sounded tight and defensive; she saw a surprised anger Jed's face. But he was looking at Perry.

Still he didn't say anything.

"Congratulations to you both," Elena murmured. "I hope you'll be happy."

"Please, don't anyone tell Father," Elizabeth said. "I'll do that myself. Shall we ride back now?"

They returned to the pens.

As they rode up, Elizabeth felt Aaron Troop's gaze rake accusingly across her face and she thought: Don't dare to say anything, you have no right. The Major rested a speculative stare on Perry, then her. He broke the silence: "I think we'd better be getting home."

"So had I," said Elena. "I can ride straight home from here." She gave Jed a quick smile. "Thank you for a very pleasant talk. I hope we'll meet again . . ."

Riding across the long flats beside the Major's buckboard, Elizabeth wondered how to approach the subject. No use trying to be circuitous; he always saw through her. Suppose that Perry was right and he'd disapprove? She'd had no reason to feel he might, yet Perry's mention of a chess game disturbed her. The Major had always cherished a theory that you could tell most of what you needed to know about a man by the way he played chess.

"Father," she said suddenly. "Perry is going to ask you for . . . your consent."

The Major said, "Whoa," expertly reining in the team till the buckboard rolled to a halt. He pulled out his pipe, struck a lucifer on his bootheel, flipped off the sparks and coaxed his pipe alight. Only then did he look at her. "That's why you came with me—to see Starbuck." He blew out the match and peered into his pipebowl. "I had my eyes open while he was convalescing. It became pretty apparent that something was developing. Do you want to marry him, Beth?"

"I'm going to," she said sharply.

"Any idea when?"

"Soon, I hope. I . . . I told him I'd discuss it with you first. Did you play chess with him?"

Major Hobart raised his brows. "Mentioned that, did he? You know, I talked with him a good deal while he was on the road to recovery."

"He holds nothing back." Aware that her voice was defensively shrill.

"No, he's forthright enough. Bright and ambitious. Yet I couldn't determine anything essential about his character—"

"So you got out the chessboard."

The Major nodded, pursing his lips. "He'd never played before. But from the outset he was bold and ingenious, willing to take chances and so damned intense about it that I doubted he was directly aware of running any risk. It landed him in some tight places at first. But he won our last two games."

"*That's* why you decided you didn't like him?"

"No, of course not. But it's when I began to really watch him and size him up." The Major thumbed back his hat. He gazed at a distant hawk hurtling down hot air currents on a glazed sky. "Beth, Perry Starbuck would dare the devil to do his worst and not think twice about it. You couldn't help getting hurt with a man like him. I don't want to see that happen."

"You liked him well enough at first!" Elizabeth said hotly "You said—"

"Don't remind me," the Major said harshly. "I was wrong. Seeing how you were starting to feel, I should have spoken up sooner. Or done something. Rather than meddle, I depended on your good sense to assert itself. You'd nursed him for weeks, been too close to him; I thought his moving to the bunkhouse would cool your perspective. A mistake, of course. I forgot that a woman in love is no more nor less than that. Too late now to point out that you're used to a style of living that's comfortable and fairly tranquil. That a life with him will be anything but. Yes," he nodded, watching her face, "way too late. All right, honey. Have any idea of his present plans? He had, as I recall, a grandiose notion of squatting in Parral country. Which is bound to bring the kind of trouble I've avoided. It would spill over onto me as his father-in-law, onto all of us at TH. Would you like to see that happen?"

"Of course not!" She kneaded her underlip between her teeth. "But suppose he could be persuaded otherwise? Suppose you offered him a future right here. A partnership in TH. I'm your heir, aren't

I? The ranch would go to me one day anyhow . . ."

Her father was already shaking his head. "No, Beth. It wouldn't work. Not with him—not the kind of man he is. I'm sorry.

"I see." Her voice was trembling; one hand fisted around her reins. "I can almost read your thoughts. Oh, I know how you think! Send me away as you'd planned, get me away from him, make me think about it some more—"

The Major sighed. "Yes, my dear, it crossed my mind. But it's a bit late for that too." He shook his head bitterly. "Starbuck! The man does everything so easily. You were always so sensible, so cool-headed, now you're just a woman in love. But why did it have to be a man like him?"

"You judge him so easily. You'll never understand. Never!"

"Oh, I understand. It's not the ranch, it's you. He saw and wanted you. Simple as that. But, honey, there's a wide cut between wanting and loving. And if he ever gets a toehold on TH, where do you think he'll be willing to stop?"

"No! I don't care what you think—"

She slashed the crop across her mount's flank, cracking him into a run. Her father's shout of "Beth!" trailed against the rush of wind in her ears and a wash of sudden blinding tears.

Chapter 7

Jed and Perry Starbuck, along with Leandro Mirabel, Rubio Perez, and Poke Tanner, were assigned to flush out the last mottes of brush on TH's southeast boundary. As they always did when far from the pens, they left the animals where they found them, tied up with rawhide *peales* till they could be brought in. Later the five men knocked off for a smoke, squatting on their heels in the chaparral.

Rubio talked about the many uses which the people of the *brasada* had found for the hides of the wild cattle that were too savage and intractable to drive. "This *peal* is of the toughest hide," he said, running one of the flinty ropes between his calloused fingers. "She come from the bull's shoulder, eh? These *chaparejos* I wear, that is softer thinner hide. My bridle, my halter, my *riata*, my saddle, these all are rawhide. Laced together, she make mattresses, tabletops, chair seats. Texas, she's held together with rawhide."

Perry was attentive. Always having an ear cocked for pieces of range lore, he asked Rubio about the curing and working of the hides. Jed only half-listened to the talk. He kept thinking back to this morning and Elena Parral, feeling a small excitement every time his thoughts touched on her pert elfin face and quick saucy chatter. It made him smile to himself.

Then he'd think of Perry and Elizabeth Hobart and the good feeling would fade. Perry had gone back on his word not to trifle with her—or so Jed had thought. When they'd gotten off alone and he'd had a chance to accuse him, Perry had said: "Kid, it's none of your business. But if it was, I can tell you that I'm not trifling with the lady's affections. I'm going all the way with her, straight to the altar."

Which had caught Jed up short. Perry meant it. But was it only the girl or was he looking beyond? Jed didn't know; he wondered if Perry knew himself. In any case, what could he do but give Perry the benefit of a doubt? He'd offered Elizabeth fair warning that night in the patio. She was going into it with her eyes open.

Leandro Mirabel, squatting beside him, nudged him with an elbow, grinning broadly. Jed turned his head. Poke Tanner had gotten up and ambled over to his horse to take a drink from his canteen on the saddle. Now he was sneaking his "rope rattler" out of a saddlebag. This was a long flexible club of woven cords about the length and thickness of a small diamondback, artfully dyed with the appropriate brown-tan-yellow markings. Even lacking a head and rattles, the damned thing was lifelike enough to startle hell out of you at a glance. Particularly when Poke would stick it up next to an unsuspecting waddy and yank a thin strong thread that lent it a quick ominous wriggle. He'd pulled the trick on Jed weeks ago, almost scaring him out of ten years' growth.

Standing behind and to the right of Perry and Rubio, Poke winked broadly at Jed and Leandro who were facing them and him, then crossed casually behind Perry and Rubio, laid the rope snake quickly down under a bush, walked a few yards on holding the attached thread and sat down. He gave the thread a surreptitious tug, pointing with his other hand.

"Hey, men! Lookit that goddam rattler . . ."

Perry glanced over his shoulder, then

twisted in one motion, the pistol blurring out of his chest holster. He fired. The rope rattler jumped about a foot. So did Poke.

He picked it up, inspected the damage and gave Perry, who was grinning as he sheathed his gun, an accusing look. "One thing I can't abide," he muttered, "it's a smart ass who sprouts eyes in the back of his head."

"Ho boy!" chortled Leandro. "I don know who jomp mos', Poke or the snake. Ai-yi!"

"Listen," Rubio said softly.

They all became quiet. Jed heard several riders coming through the brush up from the south. Wordlessly Perry eased to his feet; so did the rest of them.

In a minute three men came pushing through the chaparral. It was Augustin Parral, followed by two *vaqueros*. Jed felt his muscles tighten like cords. What would Perry do?

"Hola," Parral said. "We heard a shot."

"We are not over your line, Don Augustin," Rubio said in politely formal Spanish. By now Jed understood "border Mex" well enough to follow the gist of it.

"Did I say you were?" Augustin's smile fluted into that hint of silken cruelty as his gaze flicked again to Perry. "Blood of Christ. I did not think it possible."

109

"You might switch to English," Perry said gently. "You spoke it well enough before."

"A thousand pardons, señior. It's a barbarous accomplishment that I exercise only as required." He fingered the whip coiled on his pommel. "You cannot have forgotten the lesson I gave you. Your ugly face still bears its pretty marks."

Perry smiled and didn't answer.

Augustin looked at Rubio. "So Major Hobart hires the men who try to steal his neighbor's land."

Rubio said courteously, "I do not think he meant to give offense, señor. Also you are standing on his land."

"Here, who can be that sure of the line?" Parral's half-lidded stare slanted back at Perry. "Maybe you stand on our land. You and this gringo pig who was told to stay off it."

"Ho boy!" Leandro made a sound of flatulence with his broad lips. "If that ain' a plate of cowshit soup, hah?"

Parral gave him a cold look. "You had better hold your tongue, *vaquero,*" he snapped.

"We are on cowhunt, Don Augustin," Rubio said reasonably. "Our cows know no

110

boundaries. At cowhunt it has always been permitted."

"So? But not for this pig."

Jed had a hard time following the rapid Spanish. A moment's silence. He felt a fly settle on his cheek but didn't try to brush it away. The two *vaqueros* had their rifles out, balanced on their pommels. Jed was wearing a gun that Leandro had loaned him, insisting as to its value on-range—for dealing with anything from a sidewinder to a maddened longhorn. But he hadn't practiced with it and he only hoped this wouldn't come to gunplay . . .

"You are curiously silent, pig. Have you nothing to say?"

"I'd let it alone if I were you," Perry said mildly.

Augustin laughed. He stepped lithely down from his saddle. "Before, you snapped like a dog, gringo. Have you lost your teeth?"

"You're wasting your time." Perry's tone was dry and even. "I'm working for Hobart. I owe him something too."

"Ha, so that you will not now pay me?"

"Not while I'm working for Hobart. He wants no trouble with you people. I respect that."

"There is a possibility that you are, what do you *Yanquis* say." Parral snapped his fingers. "Chickenshit. A yellow dog without teeth. A whipped dog."

Perry shook his head, half-smiling.

Watching Parral's eyes, Jed thought dismally, he is going to crowd it all the way. Parral lifted the whip from his saddle, uncoiled it with a snap of his wrist and sent the tip flicking out. It popped a small geyser of sand over Perry's boots. He didn't move, but his head seemed to tighten into his shoulders like a ringy bull's.

"Forget it? Ah no," Parral said, "you and me, we do not forget. There are men who bide their time. You are like that. I am happy to see such patience in an American. But now it is plain to me. If we do not fight now, it must be later. When you come back to the Mora."

Perry said, "Let's get back to work, boys," and turned on his heel.

The leaded whip cracked out, ripping his right sleeve and drawing blood.

"Don't you understand, señor?" Parral whispered. "It is here. Now. Or I will whip you to your knees where you stand."

Perry had wheeled. His chest gun was ready to hand. But he didn't pull it. Maybe it was the rifle-ready *vaqueros*. Maybe something else. He said softly, "Just what do you want, Parral? Spell it out."

"I see a whip on that saddle." Parral nodded at Rubio's horse. "Is it yours, countryman? Give it to him."

Rubio silently walked to his horse; he tossed the whip to Perry. He caught it and looked at it, no expression on his face.

"If you win," Augustin said, "come to the Mora. You will not be molested."

"I think you're a crazy goddam fool," Perry murmured.

"That is what I think of you. *¿Pues y que?* So—"

He gave a dexterous backflip to his lash. Perry moved, catfooting to one side, letting Rubio's whip uncoil. Jed knew he'd never held a whip before and that it might not matter as much as Parral would think. In spite of his long-boned bulk, Perry was rawhide and spring-steel, quick as a snake.

Right now he was circling away, just watching. Augustin laughed and cracked his whip. Jed, along with Rubio, Leandro, and Poke, pulled back to the edge of the brush, giving the adversaries plenty of room. Perry hadn't held back willingly; he was as eager for the showdown as Parral. Jed had seen the same in a pair of dogs disliking each other straight off, hackles raised as they growled and circled. The issue wasn't the dominant factor. Anything at any time could set a pair like Perry and Augustin at each other's throats.

Parral swung first. But Perry, swift as the outpeeling lash, wasn't standing where the popper whacked. And then his own whip lashed out, so awkwardly that Augustin partly deflected it with his arm, grunting as its half-spent force snapped at his shoulder tip. His quick-countering cut tore Perry's other sleeve. Perry swung again, awkwardly striking too low, the lash snaking around Parral's leather-chapped leg.

It was like a soft-pedaled preliminary to what followed. The two kept apart, sending their whips curling out in powerful strokes that sounded like pistol shots. Parral's skill against Perry's evasive speed. Some of the blows landed, some didn't. It was savage, terrible, unbelievably vicious. In a few minutes both men were bleeding from slicing cuts, their clothes slashed and bloody, and Jed dimly thought it was a miracle that neither had managed to land a really lethal blow.

Parral's feral pride kept him wading in

after he realized that he'd bitten off too big a chunk. Admitting defeat short of collapse or blindness would be a blot on his honor. With Perry, Jed knew, it went even deeper: a sheer personal grit that wouldn't allow him to quit till he'd dropped in his tracks. Dogged and tough, fluid and graceful on his feet, he took what punishment he couldn't avoid while he felt his way into the battle like a boxer. It was uncanny to watch his feel for the whip improve with each stroke.

The vicious duel ended suddenly. Perry sidestepped a deft desperate cut that would have smashed the bones of his face, then flung out his free arm and let Parral's swooping lash curl around it. Perry's face twisted with pain, but his fist, already dripping blood, closed over the whip. Held it. Then he went after Augustin, landing three terrible slashing strokes.

Parral shrieked; he backed away, letting go of his immobilized whip. Then dropped to his knees, sobbing and exhausted. His *charro* jacket was cut to ribbons, mottled with blood. Perry let his arms fall to his sides. His shirt was in bloody rags; his right ear looked as if it were torn half off.

"You had enough," he said. It wasn't a question.

Parral lifted his face. His eyes swam with blood and hatred. "For now, gringo," he husked. "But I will kill you for this. I swear it."

"Is that right."

Parral swayed slowly to his feet, then started for his horse with drunken, stumbling steps. One of the *vaqueros* swung down and moved to give him a hand. Parral flung off his arm, hissing, "Get away." After three tries, he made it into the saddle.

The high-mettled Arabian was trembling and prancing with the smell of blood; his eyes rolled, his ears flattened. Augustin turned the animal's head with a savage jerk on the cruel spade bit; a slash of spurs sent him lunging away.

He poured into the chaparral at a pounding run.

Parral, reeling blindly, fought for control as they plunged through the live-oak thickets. Suddenly a whipping branch scraped him from his saddle.

The horse veered and tore free of the chaparral. He was running in the clear again, bolting away across the flinty soil and sparse thorn brush. And Parral was bouncing over the earth behind him, a foot hung in the stirrup.

"Jesus Maria!"

One *vaquero* reined his horse around, spurting in pursuit. But Rubio Perez was ahead of him. A catlike leap to his saddle and the small scarred Mexican was racing ahead of them all, overtaking the Arabian. He caught the animal as he slowed at the end of a hundred yard dash: bending low, seizing the trailing reins and pegging his pony to a halt.

Rubio had leaped down and was kneeling beside Parral as the two *vaqueros* thundered up and piled off their horses. Jed and Leandro came running after them.

Parral was screaming in a wordless high-pitched voice. His face and what showed of his body was torn to pulp. Rubio ran his small tough hands quickly over him, searching for injuries. "His arm, she is busted," he muttered.

One of the *vaqueros* bent to lift Parral.

"No, you son of a cow," Rubio said. "Wait." His hands moved some more. Then he shook his head.

"It is what I think," he said. "His back, she is broken."

The two *vaqueros* refused any help from the TH people. While one of them stayed

117

with Augustin Parral, the other headed for the Parral *hacienda* to get help and a wagon.

As soon as he'd learned what had happened, Aaron Troop lost no time. He pulled the entire crew off cowhunt and they rode back to TH headquarters in a body. Major Hobart was tramping up and down the patio, visibly upset about something. He came out to meet them, his quick glance taking them all in.

"What is it, Aaron? You're in early."

"Trouble, Major. I don't know how bad yet." Troop told it briefly, adding: "Seemed a good idea to fetch the crew in."

"You did the right thing." The Major's bleak glance slid to Perry's torn face. "Get to the kitchen, Starbuck. Ceferina will patch you up. Then I'll want to talk to you. Aaron—"

"Sir." Perry leaned across his pommel. "I wonder if I might see Elizabeth."

"She is not here." The Major was grim-jawed. "She left me as we were riding home and has not returned."

"Major, we better send some men to find her," Troop said. "She hadn't ought to be away from the place alone, if—"

"She is here," Rubio Perez broke in, seeing ahead of everyone Elizabeth's sorrel with its green-costume rider coming off the west flats.

"Men, check whatever weapons you have," Hobart said curtly. "Come with me, Aaron. We'll hold a council of war . . ."

The men were turning their horses into the corral as Elizabeth rode in. She turned pale at the sight of Perry's face. "Again," she whispered. "What happened?"

Perry told her as they walked together to the casa. Jed finished turning in their horses, then followed them to the house. As he entered the kitchen, Elizabeth and Ceferina, their sleeves rolled up, were working on Perry.

"Quit fretting over me," he told them. "It's not nearly as bad as the other time." He winked at Jed and you could tell he was enjoying the fuss. "Besides, I won."

"Nobody 'won'!" Elizabeth snapped as she jerked and tore at a strip of frayed goods, ripping it up for bandages. "Men—dear God."

Jed slacked into a chair. He wondered if "men" included her father. By now he had the impression that she and the Major had quarreled, and it wasn't hard to guess why.

"Sorry about this," Perry said.

"Don't talk foolishly. What else could you have done?" Elizabeth wiped at her eyes; she sniffed. "Men! You're all such fools . . ."

The Major and Troop were talking in the *sala,* their voices carrying faintly but clearly.

"Like I said," Troop was saying, "seems a good chance we will draw one whole hell of a lot of lightning account of this."

"Of the worst kind," Hobart answered grimly. "Have you ever been a father, Aaron?"

"Not as I know of."

"Then you can only guess at what Solano Parral is feeling. I know. A son is like an extension of your mortality, your one sure grasp on immortality, so to speak. Hell, I don't know. How do you express something that goes beyond grief? When I received news of Chad's death. And less than a month later, of Paul's . . ."

"I reckon I know, Major."

"I guess you do. You were here; you saw. The shock broke Jessica's health . . . and she never recovered. Some ways, neither did I. I'd given my parole, so I couldn't return to the war. I wanted to. Wanted to get a whole regiment of Yankees in my sights and slaughter every mother's son. That was wrong. Wrong reason, that is. But a man's lost two boys, he doesn't think. Two boys or one."

"Could be he won't lose him. Man with a busted back can recover."

"How do we know that was all of it? He was torn up badly. Might be injured internally. Anything."

"Yeh. His arm and back was all Rubio was sure of. Reckon what we do now is up to you, Major . . ."

The women finished the bandaging. Elizabeth adjusted the last fold of bandage around Perry's bare torso and tied it. He stood up, his mouth tight with pain. Both his arms were bandaged too, hiding the bruises and the freshly sewed cuts that crisscrossed scars of that other beating. His badly torn ear was stitched and bandaged.

"I need a new shirt," he said.

"You need to rest. You shouldn't be on your feet."

He touched her cheek. "I'll be all right. Thanks."

She pressed both her hands over his, holding it tight against her face She really loves him, Jed thought, and seeing the way Perry's smile reached his eyes, he knew with some

121

surprise that it was the same with his brother.

Elizabeth glanced at the litter on the table—scissors, sewing materials, a pan of bloody water, tag-ends of bandages, bloodied shreds of shirt—and said briskly to Ceferina: "Clean up the table. And burn that shirt." She looked at Perry. "You," she said, "go lie down."

Without another word, her mouth firmly set, she walked out to the *sala* where her father and Troop were talking. "The situation couldn't be plainer," the Major was saying. "A man like Don Solano, proud as all hell . . ."

"An eye for an eye, is that it?" Elizabeth said clearly.

A pause. Then Hobart said: "I think so, honey. I can only guess, but it seems certain he'll come here. And not alone. He'll want the man who whipped his son. Beat him so badly he fell off his horse and got dragged half to death."

Perry gave Jed a faint crooked smile. "They're talking about me, I believe."

"Us," Jed said. "Maybe we'd better get in on this."

They walked to the *sala* beyond the dining room, pausing by the bead portieres that framed the connecting doorway. Troop was sitting uncomfortably on a low settee, hat resting on his knees. The Major was pacing the carpet in a slow circle, head bent. White-faced, Elizabeth was facing them both.

"Father," she was saying vehemently, "Perry didn't provoke the fight! Augustin Parral did, and what he got . . ."

"He deserved? Maybe. I'm no judge. But I know how Parral feels."

Perry mildly cleared his throat. They all looked at him and there was a moment's silence.

"Major," Troop said softly, "that old man wants Starbuck and he don't get him, it's going to cut all hell loose."

"What do you suggest?" Elizabeth said hotly. "That we turn Perry over to him?"

Troop ran a hand over his burrlike hair. "I ain't saying that. All I'm saying if this ain't handled right, a lot of good men could get killed. You never seen a war start up between two big outfits, I ain't going to try to tell you what it's like. Just a couple things. They all start from a mite of a squabble like this. And they don't stop with no right-off ruckus."

"What you're saying," Hobart said curtly,

"is we surrender, Starbuck or fight, there's no third choice."

"Sure. One. Give him a sack of grub and a fast horse."

"Father." Elizabeth's voice was tightly controlled. "Perry is hurt. He certainly can't ride far or fast and he doesn't know the country. Parral will have trackers who do."

Hobart sighed. "And if we try to hide him somewhere . . ."

"Major," Troop said, "you hide him here, or some'eres near here, it's all the same. Parral wouldn't take nobody's word on it, he would insist on searching the place. He don't find him here, he'll hunt him out. We get in his way, it's all the same too."

Hobart tugged his beard, frowning. "Seems we haven't a wide gallery of choices, then. In any case—"

"Father!" Elizabeth thrust the word like a knife. "If you let anything happen to Perry, I'll never forgive you. Never!"

She whirled and ran from the room, past Jed and Perry. Hobart called, "Wait a minute, honey," but the door of her bedroom slammed.

Perry said quietly, "Much ado about nothing, Major. I've decided to leave. It's the best thing all around."

"Under ordinary circumstances," Hobart said grimly, "I couldn't agree with you more."

Perry grinned. "I'll be coming back—for Beth. When I do, I'll be in a position to stand up to the Parrals."

"Will you?" the Major said sardonically. "Well, forget it. You're staying here."

"I can't do that, Major."

"You've no choice," Hobart said curtly. "In no shape to ride. Ignorant of the country. How far would you get?"

"I can't say. But if I can keep ahead of 'em awhile, it'll lead any fight away from here. Away from all of you."

Hobart eyed him narrowly. "Is that really important to you?"

"It's my fight, not yours. I don't want any other lives jeopardized on my account. Particularly Beth's and Jed's."

"Aside from them—is it humanity or just pride, Starbuck?" the Major asked dryly.

"Pride. I owe you people enough; the debt is already topheavy. Involving you in my fight would be a poor way to pay off." Perry grinned crookedly. "You'll recognize that as another point of pride, Major."

"I have mine too, Starbuck. You're not leaving here."

"Think you can stop me?"

125

"With one order. I can have you hogtied."

Perry threw back his head and laughed. "What you really want—be honest, Major—is to see me far away from here. And I'm not so eager to die young I can't see the only chance I have of staying alive is staying here. We're at odds against our own best interests, you and I. And we can't help ourselves. Funny thing, pride."

"It's a little more than that, Starbuck. All right, there's Beth. She'd never forgive me, she meant it. But if you were any other man on my crew, I'd do the same. Even if you were a stranger to me and I was damned sure you were in the right—which you are—I wouldn't act a jot differently."

"In your place," Perry smiled, "I'm afraid I would. I'm no Christian gentleman. Just an honest sinner who pays off his notes. That's a difference between us."

"There's another too. I can back up what I say."

"Holding me here by having me trussed up like a hog?"

"If necessary."

Perry laughed. "Well, I won't make it necessary." He winked at Jed. "A man needs his hands free to hold a gun. Assuming you'll let me help defend myself . . ."

Chapter 8

They waited in the sweltering afternoon heat.

Major Hobart and Troop had agreed that Don Solano could muster a force twice the size of theirs. So they concentrated on the defense of the main house and prepared for a state of siege behind ancient adobe walls that wore bullet scars from early day Indian raids.

Men were stationed at windows in each room. They were armed with everything from old muskets to breech-loading rifles, from cap-and-ball Colts to the cartridge-firing Smith & Wessons. Three big barrels were brought into the house and filled with water carried in buckets from the outside well. If Parral chose to attempt a drag-out siege, they had enough food, water, and ammunition to last a couple of weeks.

The men squatted on their heels, smoking, talking quietly.

Elizabeth and Ceferina had gone through the rooms and collected vases and gimcracks and other breakables, transferring these to the root cellar. Elizabeth ordered the carpets rolled up and carried down to the cellar along with fragile pieces of furniture. The men obliged, chuckling over female foo-feraw, amused by the tin plates the women placed by each window to catch their ashes. But they were careful to use them.

Their spirits were high, no complaining. In a country where organized law didn't amount to shucks, Jed had learned that guidelines of loyalty, friendship, and crude justice were strictly observed and never questioned. A man expected to fight for his brand when it became necessary, knowing his outfit would stand back of him or any of his bunkies in a rightful dispute. Perry was in the right, Hobart right in defending him; that was all they had to know.

Jed, Perry, and Leandro Mirabel crouched by a front window of the *sala* facing on the patio. The squat wall that squared off the patio made it the hardest position to defend: the only place where an enemy could run up to close cover.

"Leastways," said Poke Tanner who was stationed by another window, " 'dobe don't burn, should they take it in mind to smoke us out."

"Roof, she ain' adobe," grinned Leandro. "How you like that, *amigo?*"

"Aw, shut up. Christ!"

Jed shifted on his heels, gazing out the window. A flinty flicker-dance of heat glanced off the valley floor. "Perr," he said, and Perry looked at him. "If you'd left, I'd have gone with you. You couldn't have stopped me."

Perry chuckled. "Don't bet on it. But thanks."

Hobart and his range boss came in from the next room, conferring in low voices.

"Well," Troop was saying, "I don't think it will make one whole hell of a lot of difference. But all right. It is your play."

"Can't do any harm to try, Aaron. If there's even one chance of heading off a fight . . ." The Major brushed a hand over his beard. "Partly, it'll depend on how badly Parral's son was injured. For the rest, I can talk to him as a man who's felt what he's feeling. That may count for something, maybe not. But I mean to try."

Troop gave a pessimistic grunt. "You just be damn' careful."

Rubio Perez, squinting through a window, said: "Major, is someone coming."

Horsebackers were swinging into sight from behind an arm of hills, spreading out in a tight line as they came nearer. They moved at a trot, dust spraying up around their mounts' legs. Jed counted up to thirty men and more.

"You didn't guess wrong, Major," Troop muttered. "Got his whole crew behind him or I'm a banana-tailed muley cow."

Jed's mouth was dry, his hands sweating around his rifle. His eyes ached with heat and tension. Don't be so damned young, he told himself disgustedly. A hand gripped his arm and he glanced at Leandro who merely winked and then took his hand away.

It was more steadying than many words.

Funny, Jed thought, how Leandro and he had grown as close as brothers in a lot of small ways that counted, ways he'd never known with Perry.

The body of riders stopped a couple of hundred yards away. They held a rigid line as two of them came on toward the house. Jed recognized one, a big hog-faced man, as Tito Rozales, the Parral *segundo*. The man beside him rode a splendid Arabian bay. Young Augustin's horse or its twin. Then they were close up, halting beyond the wide gate that pierced the patio wall, and Jed knew from the silver-trimmed saddle that this was Augustin's mount all right.

The man who rode him was tall and slender, with a lined eagle face and fierce mustaches. An old man for sure, seventy or so, but he sat his seat with the firm straight-backed ease of a boy. Watching him made you realize just how thin the Parral blood had run in his son. He swept off his sombrero like an old-time cavalier, sun blazing on his silvery plume of hair.

"There's a man," Perry muttered.

"Hobart!" called Solano Parral. "Major Hobart!"

The Major clamped on his hat and crossed to the door. He was in his shirtsleeves, a pistol belted at his hip. He paused, hand on the latch, and glanced at the men by the windows. "Gentlemen," he said quietly, "there will be no shooting except on Mr. Troop's order. Aaron, use your best judgment. I'm depending on you."

"Look, Major," Troop said, "you can talk as easy from in here."

"No. It's between Parral and me, man to man. If what I say is to carry any force, I have to go out there and face him. Otherwise it won't mean a damned thing."

"He's got Rozales."

"No. You'll stay here, Aaron. It's only a parley. But if something should happen, it

131

can't happen to both of us. There'll be a fight to lead then."

Troop nodded reluctantly. "Just watch yourself damn' close. That's one touchy old bastard."

"Sir." Perry got to his feet. "If you're going to expose yourself, I feel it's my responsibility to side you out there."

"Sorry," Hobart said dryly. "I don't aim to conduct a peace parley with a walking provocation beside me. You'd be a red flag, Starbuck. Stay where you are and under no circumstances show yourself."

The Major raised the latch as Elizabeth came quickly into the room, holding her rustling skirts. "What was that about a parley? Father, what are you doing?"

"I'm going out to talk with Parral. Watch her, Aaron."

Hobart went out the door as he spoke. Troop closed it behind him and loomed before it as Elizabeth, her face distraught, started forward. He shook his head. "You stay in here." She stood biting her lip, then moved over to Perry and slipped her hand into his. Troop eyed them both coldly, then looked away.

They watched Hobart start across the patio. Don Solano and Rozales paced their horses through the gate, iron shoes ringing on the flagstones. When the Major halted close to the *ramada*-shaded bench, they stopped too, about twenty feet from him.

"My son's back is broken, Major Hobart," Parral said in clear, slightly lisping English. "He cannot move his legs."

"I'm sorry."

"Do you hear me, Major Hobart?" Don Solano's voice rose slightly. "Below the break, there is no feeling in my son's body. He cannot walk. He will not walk again."

"I heard you, Don Solano. Sometimes this thing is temporary."

The don's mustaches quivered. He looked toward the men at the windows. "I know Aaron Troop and the Mexicans. The rest I do not know. Is one of them the man?"

"I don't know what your *vaqueros* told you," Hobart said, "but this thing was not my man's fault. I know your feeling. I lost two sons—"

"You are lucky. Your sons, more so. Can you deny it? You are a man, like me. We have lost wives, we have grieved. Your sons are dead. All that is *nada*, it is finished. My son lives on. In a body that is dead."

"Maybe not. The spine must be damaged,

133

but such an injury may heal. Also there are doctors, specialists. I can send for—"

"I do not bargain!" Parral tight-reined his prancing bay. "A man who is in the right does not bargain, Major Hobart. I want that man."

"Parral, use your head!" The Major's voice turned cold and furious. "Man, we're prepared to meet anything you can throw against us. My man was not at fault. Do you think I'll deliver him to be killed? As to bargaining, I'll strike any bargain necessary to avoid bloodshed."

Parral shook his head. "There is no middle ground. We are neighbors and we are at peace, you and me. Or we are enemies. Which is it?"

"It isn't that simple. It can't be."

A queer smile twisted Parral's lips. "I have read of a thing your people—in northern Europe, eh? —had long ago. For a death, payment in gold by the killer's family. This, it is said, satisfied the family of the deceased. Cold metal for a life. This was called justice. You are strange, you barbarians of the north. You war, you kill, yet you claim to reverence life. But we are Latins. We carry our lives on the tips of our fingers, lightly. It is a grand drama we live. We do not haggle with its terms. A life for a life."

"Don Solano, I cannot believe what you say. You are a learned man, a reasonable man. For many years we have respected one another's rights and boundaries . . ."

"Only blood will settle this," Parral broke in harshly. "Will it be the blood of one or the blood of many? Give me that man, Major Hobart. Or what happens will be on your head."

"You have a fine way of turning the case to suit your—drama," Hobart said softly. "I will not play your game."

Don Solano jerked his reins, starting to wheel the Arabian away.

"Wait." The Major's voice was hard and even. "You talk of blood for blood. Why should others die for one man's quarrel? I have a daughter in this house."

"Send her out. She will not be harmed."

"It'd not enough. There are good men who will die. So let's settle it in your way. But here. Now. I challenge you, *mano a mano.*"

Parral curbed his horse, his fierce eyes impatient. "My quarrel is not with you."

"You have said it. We're peaceful neighbors or we're enemies. If you want to fight, then by God it's me you'll fight. Me alone."

Hobart deliberately lifted his gun from its holster, forcing the issue yet giving Parral all the time he might need. The don gave a blurred oath, then dropped his hand to the silver-inlaid Colt at his hip. The two guns came up, the shots blasted across each other in an overlapping roar.

Hobart was smashed off his feet, falling backward on the flagstones. Don Solano's body was almost jolted from his saddle. He held onto the pommel, coughing. Blood poured from his mouth and spilled over the white ruffles of his shirt. Then he rocked sideways and fell. His gun clattered across the stones.

"Father!" Elizabeth screamed.

She whirled for the door, but Troop barred her way and Perry caught her by the arms and pulled her back. "Hold her," Troop said as he went out the door.

Tito Rozales was off his horse, shouting something at the shifting line of *vaqueros*. He was telling them to hold back, to hold their fire. Troop had halted as Rozales spoke and now both he and Rozales moved toward the bodies.

Jed, like the others, was tense with shock.

No sound in the room but Elizabeth's choked sobbing.

Tito turned Don Solano's body over on its back. After a minute he looked up. "The *patrón* is dead," he said in a hushed, formal tone.

"So's the Major." Troop straightened up from his inspection and looked squarely at Tito Rozales.

"*Dios,* why must such a thing be? These were both men. *Muy hombres.*" The *segundo*'s great-jowled face was puckered with restrained grief. "I do not want to fight you, señor."

"No." Troop shook his head, looking at the flagstones. "There's enough blood right here . . ."

Chapter 9

Troy Hobart was buried on a spot he had chosen long ago. Beside his wife on a deep-grassed rise several hundred yards from the house. Men of his crew lowered the simple wooden box into the grave and filled it and set a wooden marker at the head of the mound. They stood with bowed heads while Aaron Troop, holding Elizabeth's small Bible in his hands, carefully and fumblingly read the Major's favorite passage from Job. Job the man of sorrows, Elizabeth thought dully as she listened. I never thought of Father as a sorrowing man. But yes, he must have been, those last years . . .

The ceremony over, she returned to the house alone. She wanted to be alone, she thought. But the silence and emptiness of the *casa*, even the lingering smell of his tobacco in the rooms, depressed her. Ceferina, who had gone to the deserted old chapel to pray for her patron's soul, soon returned. Her red-eyed snuffling as she went about her work wore on Elizabeth's nerves till she retreated out to the patio with a basket of sewing. She sat on the bench under the *ramada* and tried to concentrate on some crocheting. But a sick grief kept lumping in her throat and she set the work aside and stared at the sun-wrinkled flagstones. They were washed clean of the brown stains, but she kept seeing them. *Why?* He was so fine a man, so good. It wasn't his time, he wasn't ready to die . . .

She heard footsteps cross the patio and looked up. Perry was there, hat in hand. "Beth," he said.

She smoothed her black taffeta skirt with her hands, trying to bite back tears. "I was just wondering why," she whispered. "But I guess I know. It was because of the kind of man he was. He couldn't do anything else."

He sat beside her, gazing at the flagstones. He shook his head. "Be a liar if I told you I understand. I don't."

"How could you? There was nobody like him. He knew exactly what he was doing and that it had to be done that way. Giving Solano Parral an even chance because it was the only way to narrow the fight to them alone and end it, then and there. To save the lives of young men on both sides, men with their lives ahead of them. I know so well the way he thought! By his lights he couldn't do anything less. Could you ever understand a man like that, Perry?"

"Maybe not. I never claimed the role of Christian gentleman, Beth. It was your father's part, one he filled well."

"And foolishly—by your lights."

"No. I can be head-on with a man and respect him for what he is, not what he believes. I felt the same way about old Parral and he wanted my scalp."

"And I don't understand *that*."

They were silent awhile. The cottonwoods drowsed in the heat, their leaves motionless. He reached for her hand and held it tightly. "Beth. If you want to call it off, I'll understand."

"Did I say I did?"

He lifted and settled his shoulders. "It was my doing that led to it, wasn't it?"

"Oh Perry." Shaking her head tiredly. "I've spent hours trying to understand it all. It was simply a chain of events . . . you, Augustin Parral, his father, my father, the kind of men you all were and the way things happened. You can't be faulted on intent. You tried to leave, draw the danger away, and Father wouldn't let you."

"Thank you for being so levelheaded . . . about everything." He scrubbed a hand over his jaw. "You know everything about me that's important to know. The best with the worst. From your standpoint anyway, some of it can't be too pleasant. I won't be the easiest man in the world to live with and that's God's truth. But I love you. That's the truth too."

"I love you, Perry."

"Then let's be married now. Not a proper suggestion, but I've never pretended to be a proper man. You need somebody now. Not a year or six months from now. You need me."

"Yes." She leaned toward him, a choking in her throat. "I do need you, Perry. Very much."

His hands were strong and positive as they pulled her close. She stiffened against a wave of doubt: not of her feelings, but of what the living force of this man would mean in her life. Nothing will be as it was, she thought. And then, in the security of his arms, she ceased to think.

Three days later they drove to Moratown in a two-seat buckboard, accompanied by Jed and Ceferina. The latter two stood by as witnesses while the Methodist circuit rider performed a brief ceremony. Afterward they returned to TH. Jed, wedged into the rear seat beside the housekeeper's bulk, was glum and silent. Something had to be said and he didn't know how to approach it.

Sunset was reddening the horizon as they unhitched and turned in the horses. By now the crew was in, and Perry invited Aaron Troop to the house for a drink. As soon as he, Perry, and Jed were seated alone in the *sala*, Troop in his dusty range clothes, the brothers still wearing wrinkled suits,

Perry laid it out for the range boss in blunt words.

"You ramrodded for the Major a long time, didn't you, Aaron?"

"Thirteen year," Troop said stonily.

Glass in hand, Perry paced the floor in a slow circle, his big frame restless with leonine energy. "I have a lot to learn. I'll need a man with your kind of experience and know-how. If we can get along, I'd like the man to be you. Just make no mistake. I'll be running this spread now and I'll run it my way. Once I take hold, things will be a hell of a lot different here."

Troop was seated on the horsehair divan, elbows on his knees, staring at the hat dangling from his hands. His drink rested untasted on the floor by his boot. He nodded without looking up. "Figured they'd be."

"The Major had a good thing that he never made the most of," Perry continued. "There's room to spread out, land for the taking and plenty of unbranded stock running wild on it. For years Hobart salted away his money, clear profit that should have been put to work developing and expanding. So much of it that we're in shape to double our operation at once. I intend to. I'm going to hire more men and set up an outfit in the country north of here. That's just a start. When the time comes, I'll gain title to that and enough additional land to triple our holdings."

Troop's cold eyes lifted. "You ready to fight for it too?"

"If I have to. In the courts if possible, but any way necessary." Perry's lips curled up genially at the corners. "If that's too rich for your blood, say so now."

"I'll stick."

"You haven't liked me much from the start, have you, Troop?"

"I ain't obliged to."

Perry nodded pleasantly. "That's right. I know why you don't. Same reason you didn't quit cold after the Major was killed. All right, that's fine, how you feel about my wife is your business. It doesn't even worry me."

Jed's muscles flinched instinctively. That sort of kick-in-the-teeth candor was typical of Perry, but how would Troop take it? A slow flush darkened the range boss's face; his fists crushed the hatbrim. Abruptly he stood up and started for the door.

"Just a minute," Perry said. "About the Major's idea, sending one herd to New Orleans, another to this new place in Kansas, Abilene. What do you think of it?"

Troop turned, settling his weight on his heels. His face was twitching, but his voice held quiet. "Major never throwed all his chips in one pot. New Orleans drive'll cut the gamble."

"And the stakes. I've gone over the ranch books; we can afford to gamble. I've seen the Kansas Pacific tracks and the Eastern markets are crying for beef. It's a dead-sure profit, a fat one. Two herds. Mirabel will boss one, Perez the other. Both to Abilene."

Troop shrugged. "Whatever you want."

Perry moved to the sideboard, picked up the Major's humidor and emptied out the Havanas in his hand. He walked over to Troop and held them out. "Divvy these up with the boys. I don't like cigars."

Troop hung on his heels a moment, his feelings plain on his face. It was one last chance to pick up the gage so obviously flung down. Then he took the cigars, pocketed them and walked out.

"You'd better go easy with Troop," Jed said sharply. "He's no man to play games with."

Perry grinned. "Agreed. But you'll learn it's best to square things away with a man.

Saves misunderstandings later. Want another drink?"

"No." Jed hesitated. "Perr, this is as good a time as any to say it. I think the time's come for me to move on."

"Wondered when you'd come out with that." Perry walked to the sideboard and refilled his glass. "It's out of the question. You stay."

Jed scowled. "Dammit, you're a settled man now. You've found what you were looking for. All of it. And I . . ."

Perry strode to the door that opened on the bedroom corridor. "Beth!" he called. When Elizabeth came from her room, where she'd changed from her bouffant velvet wedding gown to a plain gingham frock, he put his arm around her and said: "This jughead wants to pull stakes on us. Would you tell him what we've discussed? What we decided on together?"

"We want you to stay, Jed," Elizabeth said gravely. "You're the only family we have now."

"Time might remedy that." Perry winked and gave her waist a squeeze. "Thing is, boy, we'd take it right unkindly if you walked out on us. Why not throw in with TH? Invest your share of our money in the outfit. All the undeveloped potential here, we'll be growing fast. You can grow along with us."

"I don't know," Jed said guardedly. "I haven't decided on anything for sure. When I do, I might find out this isn't for me."

"Then," Perry said promptly, "you'll say the word and I'll buy out your per cent for whatever it's then worth. Meantime your money'll be earning more for you. I'm gambling, though, that you'll want to stick."

"Could be," Jed said self-consciously. "The life's sort of grown on me."

"That's a 'yes,' " Perry said. "Let's all drink to it." He filled three glasses at the sideboard.

Elizabeth smiled. "As a partner and one of the family now, you'll be giving more orders than you take. But I've one more order for you, Jed."

"Yes, ma'am."

"Move your things out of the bunkhouse and in here . . ."

As Jed threw his plunder together, he was aware of the crew's silent, appraising stares. But he wasn't immediately concerned about their reactions. None of the impressive plans that Perry had discussed included encroachment on Parral land. Apparently his new position on TH had deflected his ambitions into other channels.

For now, Jed thought. For how long?

The qualification bothered him. But maybe it was groundless. Anyway his agreement with Perry provided him with a sure out if he ever needed one.

Taking along Poke Tanner and Jimmy Velasco, two crewmen who knew the country and its people, Perry went up to Moratown again. He spent a couple of days there introducing himself around, buying drinks, striking up dozens of acquaintances, asking hundreds of questions.

Meantime his mind was filing away countless bits of information about the land, its climate, its people, its politics. No detail was too small or insignificant to escape his notice. He ordered enormous quantities of supplies to be freighted to TH and established lenient credit terms with merchants. Afterward, guided by the two crewmen, he visited backwoods ranches, roadhouses, and cantinas. While familiarizing himself with everything he could, he saw that the word was spread everywhere: TH was hiring men and paying top wages.

It was nearly two weeks before the three

of them returned, but before then men vere drifting daily into TH headquarters wanting to hire on. Following instructions that Perry had left, Jed signed them all up. When Perry and his companions finally rode in, both Tanner and Velasco were in a state of exhaustion; each had shed a good ten pounds of weight.

Next evening, after both had slept the clock around, they sat in the cookshack and stowed away a huge meal and told the rest of the crew about the trip.

"Jesus Christ, I never see the beat of that man," Poke told them between mouthfuls. "He's a goddam tornado when he gets going and he don't never stop going. He run the pair of us ragged. Never got more'n three hours shut-eye at a stretch, then he was up'n'off again. Done what sleeping we could in the saddle. Not much. We be way out somewhere and he'd yell, 'Poke, what's this called?' Some goddam plant he wants the name of. If I know it I tell him, then he has Jimmy tell him the Spanish name. Makes Jimmy talk nothing to him but border spick so's he can pick it up faster. Questions, questions, questions! And Christ, he don't forget nothing. Got the medicine tongue too. No matter he's a greenhorn and a Yank to the

Anglos, a goddam gringo to the Mex, he fetches a man's fancy like a dead cow fetches flies and leaves 'em all grinning. Never see the beat of him."

Aaron Troop, stony-faced silent till now, looked up from his plate. "He's doing fine," he said. "All the grease he totes, he'll never wear out no wheels getting where he's going."

"Where's 'at, Aaron?" asked a crewman.

"Likely Hell."

Troop did not smile. And Poke thought his eyes looked god awful funny as he said it.

Chapter 10

With another full crew to replace the men on drive, Perry wasn't slowing down any. He invited Aaron Troop to supper at the *casa*. Afterward, over coffee and brandy, he discussed his plans, pacing the floor around the table as he talked. They'd get a cowhunt under way at once; no reason they couldn't send another herd north this season.

"You got two herds on the trail now," Troop argued. "That's enough risk to have riding on a drive that ain't been tried before.

Even if you know the best route to follow, allowing for time of year and weather and river crossings and so on, there's plenty of reconstructed Injuns and jayhawker gangs to run a gamut of before you hit the Kansas border. Then there's free-soil farmers scared of fever . . ."

"Beth tells me it was you who first talked up Abilene to the Major. Not going back on your own judgment, are you?"

"The Major cut his odds just right. One herd, an early start north. First herds in will fetch the big prices."

"Of course, but we can afford to take extra chances. We have all the men we need to work out miles of brush that haven't been touched by cowhunters in many years, if ever. Poke and Jimmy and I covered a good deal of it on our way back. It's crawling with wild cattle."

Perry walked to the window and stared out, his back to the room. Jed glanced at Elizabeth as she sipped her coffee and said nothing. Like him, she'd learned that Perry's way left little room for comment. He'd occasionally mention how green he was to the game and his need to defer to experienced judgment, but while he absorbed cold facts like a sponge, he ignored all ad-

150

vice. He made every decision himself, and once it was made, all hell couldn't pry him loose from it.

As Jed had expected, Perry had taken over TH with great ease. Several older hands had quit, vowing they'd never work for a man who'd "marry in" with the Major hardly cold in his grave. But with most of the crew, Perry's warm personal touch had dispelled all doubts. Just one more side to his unshakable confidence which nothing seemed to dent. That was hard to take offense at because, like his cool easy talents, it was a completely unself-conscious part of him . . .

He turned from the window, his lips pursed speculatively. "Aaron, tomorrow I want you to take ten of the men and set up a camp down by the Mora. We'll work the brush north from there up."

So there it was.

Jed had wondered when it would come, even while hoping against hope it wouldn't. He wadded his napkin and laid it beside his plate. "Perr, you know better than anyone that's inside the Parral claim."

"And you know I don't recognize their claim."

Elizabeth stared at her husband. "You can't mean that."

"I'm not in the habit of saying what I don't mean."

"But you promised me . . . !"

"Gave you my word I wouldn't settle on the Mora. No question of that now. I said nothing about working that piece for cows."

"Perry, Father gave his life to head off trouble with the Parrals! If you do this . . ."

"What Parrals?" Perry's smile was iron-tinged. "The don is dead, he was the big rooster. The young one? I'd say his spurs are pretty well clipped."

"He's still got a voice," Troop said. "He can still give orders. He's got a *segundo* to see they're carried out."

"That scare you, Aaron?"

"Yeah, it scares me. Anyone it don't scare is a plain damned fool."

There was a long silence in the room. Perry broke it softly: "I want to say just three things. First, if every scrap of old Spanish parchment disputing claim to a chunk of Texas were honored, we might as well hand the whole damned state back to Spain. There are also hundreds of cross-claims and counter-claims and the only ones that carry any weight are those that have enough dollars or enough bullets to back them. Possession is nine-tenths of the law. So what in hell gives the Parrals special license to kick up a fuss about an arbitrary line? Second, I consider that I paid damned rough dues for the right to work cattle out of that Mora strip. I got an outfit burned for it and I have scars to show what else I got. Third" —he directed a stare at Troop— "I'll say it again. Any time the game spooks you, cash in. Tuck your tail between your legs and run."

Troop colored; his eyes squinted half-shut. "I ain't in the habit of running from whatever. You want to step outside a minute, I will show you."

The cold challenge left Perry's face; he laughed. "Now what would that prove? That he who fights best is right? I'm not afraid of you, you're not afraid of me. So we've nothing to prove. But I'll apologize if you'll feel better."

"I got nothing to prove to you, that's damn' sure," Troop muttered.

He sounded angry with himself. Jed knew the feeling. Perry played your feelings like a hooked fish and never let his own get involved. But it was foolish of him, Jed thought, to make Troop look the fool in front of Elizabeth. It could only aggravate the deep hatred Troop must already feel for

153

him. Yet it was a game that Perry couldn't seem to resist playing.

"Of course you haven't," Perry said, boyishly smiling and infectiously genial now. "It'll be a long day tomorrow. I suggest we all turn in . . ."

Before he went to his room, Jed drew Perry aside. "I suppose it would be a waste of words to advise that you consider this move some more."

"You just said it." Perry's blue-green gaze was amused. "Unless you know a new argument.'"

"Just the old one. Good sense."

"What you call good sense meant scraping along on a busted-down farm. Somehow I find this better." Perry shrugged. "If you're scared, my offer stands—"

"I'm scared," Jed said. "But not for me. For you, Perr."

A momentary surprise flickered in Perry's face. Then he laughed and slapped Jed on the shoulder. "You're a goddamned old woman. Go on to bed."

When she and Cefetina had finished the after-dinner chores, Elizabeth retired to the master bedroom. Usually she liked to sit up with Perry, going over the account or tally books with him. Or just talking. He was a good if single-minded conversationalist; he had a fantastic range of knowledge, but his real interests focused almost exclusively on industry and economics and politics. Local, state, and national, in that order. He was a fascinating raconteur, he had no reservations about sharing his thoughts and plans with her. Though she'd usually get the feeling he was talking things out to clarify them for his own use and didn't really care whether she listened or not.

Still it was a total sharing, a close and contented relationship, the kind she'd hoped and dreamed of finding with a man. And the invariable period to all talk: the force of love welling up like a sweet choking when, unable to wait any longer, she'd whisper: "I'm ready for bed. Aren't you?" And he'd laugh and carry her to their room and their lovemaking would be fierce and consuming and drain them both to completion. The frustration of his two weeks' absence had been maddening.

But tonight she was upset. After she'd changed to her nightgown and peignoir, she sat at her pier table, looking blankly at herself in the mirror, not even keeping count of strokes as she brushed her hair. The happiness she'd felt had quickly blunted the fact of her father's death to a dull ache. Perhaps it had been a good thing, yet thinking of it now made her feel almost shamed. Perry's sudden-announced intent to cowhunt on the Mora strip brought back a swarm of doubts that she'd thought had been put to rest.

Had Perry really been honest with her?

You couldn't say he'd truly lied; she'd extracted no promise from him regarding the Mora strip except not to settle it. Fault of omission? Maybe the real fault was hers. She'd unthinkingly shunned any further consideration of the related events that had led to her father's death. Too painful yet, too recent. She'd assumed that the agreement between Troop and Rozales would end the trouble, that Perry would he satisfied to let sleeping dogs lie. But prudence wasn't one of Perry's virtues. His love of the long chance, the reckless gamble, disturbed and alarmed her, accustomed as she was to her father's careful restraint. Being used to a strong man in her life, though, she hadn't felt it was her place to question.

But something like this . . . how could she just ignore it? She looked around the big room that had been her father's, full of things he had known and touched, feeling a quality of accusation in them. She felt the stab of sudden, lonely grief. Father, what'll I do? Tell me . . .

She took a grip on herself. Leaned forward, studying herself in the mirror, lamplight making tawny shimmers on her darkly red hair. A woman's weapons, she thought. The most potent of all weapons. If she couldn't turn a man with these, how much of a woman was she?

She resumed the slow brush strokes. The door opened and Perry entered. He closed the door, shucked off his coat and hung it up, then tugged at his tie.

"Perry."

"Yes?"

"About the Mora strip, I understand how you feel. But do we *need* to work that area? I mean, we're branching out north and east and we can't develop our holdings much farther without overextending ourselves. At least not at present. Can we?"

He turned a cold, quiet glance on her. "Let's put our cards on the table. Say what's really bothering you."

"Haven't I said it? The trouble between you and the Parrals was settled, my father died to settle it. I think Tito Rozales must have convinced Augustin and his sister that it's to everyone's interest to leave it that way. Must we stir up another hornet's nest?"

He moved up behind her and laid his hands on her shoulders. "You don't understand, do you? It's a man's thing, Beth. I'm not out to buy trouble or to rob anyone. I won't touch a Parral-branded critter or do anything to prevent their stock from ranging that strip as freely as ours. But I paid my dues for equal rights. I mean to have 'em."

"Is that how most men think?"

He shrugged; his voice turned sandy with irritation. "Not my concern. It's how *I* think. If you wanted to play life out your pa's way, you married the wrong man."

"Do you think the Parrals will see it your way? Or isn't that your concern either, that this, this foolishness could lead to violence—killing—"

"Violence?" He pulled her around to face him. "Honey, you want to talk about principles and violence, a half million men died in the late war over a little question of the rights of states. Always something to die over, that's the nature of men, it hasn't changed any since they lived in caves and tangled over the prime hunting grounds.

You lost two brothers in the war, your pa fought in it, did they question—"

"There *is* a difference, Perry," she said hotly. "All the difference in the world—"

"Is there? Well, I fought on the other side" —his lips pushed out sardonically— "because I was young and busting full of ideals such as the preservation of the Union. Was I right? Your pa and brothers didn't think so. Me, I don't know any more who was right. And it sure as hell doesn't matter to the men who died. Right or wrong, Yank or Reb, they're just as dead. You want to know all that I believe in?" His hands left her shoulders; he straightened. "What a man feels inside. Just that. What he needs and has got to have or dry up and quit living. It's the only certain faith he can tie to. Call it selfish if you want. Or a lack in my character. But I can't walk in your father's steps, I can't follow any way but my own."

"I understand," she murmured. "I won't say any more."

She rose with a hiss of silk and faced him. Slipped off the peach-colored peignoir and let it drop. "I love you. Nothing else is important." Whispering it. Seeing his eyes kindle with the quick dry lights. Feeling a quiet triumph in her woman's weapon.

She moved against him, twisting her mouth against his in a fierce kiss spiced by the delicate dart of her tongue. His arms circled her and tightened. After a moment she pulled her head back, whispering, "I'm ready for bed. Aren't you?"

Chapter 11

"Way he carries on," said Poke Tanner, "you'd think he's God A'mighty hisself. Only you wait, he's gonna overreach hisself."

"You think so, hey?" said Jimmy Velasco.

"Hell yes, he's come too far too fast. I never see nothing like it. He can't keep it up. He's gonna overreach hisself and the whole goddam thing is gonna rattle down like a house of cards."

"Huh. Maybe you right."

"Yeah." Poke grinned. "Sure one hell broth of fun watching him build up to it, though. Starbuck got more ideas going than a dog got fleas. You keep wondering what he is gonna come up with next."

Jimmy cleared his throat in sharp warning. Poke threw a quick look over his shoulder; Jed was riding a few yards to his left and back. He had ranged forward unnoticed by Poke, but hadn't intended to eavesdrop. Since moving his things into the main house, he had felt shut out of the crew's easy camaraderie.

Jed, Poke, Jimmy, and several other crewmen were pushing a last bunch of cows north toward the Tuley Spring pens. For over a week, they'd been working out the brushlands above the Mora River deep inside the old Parral claim. Riding together at all times and keeping their eyes open for trouble as well as cows. When a week had passed and trouble hadn't come, they'd relaxed a little but not much. The only times that TH crews had ever cowhunted this far south were in conjunction with Parral crews, by agreement of Major Hobart and Solano Parral.

Of late, occasionally sighting Parral riders, they'd known their movements were being watched and reported. Still no countermove by the Parral camp. Himself crippled, his father dead, Augustin Parral might be skittish of again tangling horns with Perry. Or he might merely be biding his time.

Jed fervently hoped not. He also hoped that Perry had made all the point he needed to. That his unanswered challenge to Parral

161

would satisfy him. Just as he hoped that Elizabeth would be a gentling, steadying influence in Perry's life. But it was too soon to tell. And when could you be sure of anything where Perry was concerned?

Coming onto the flats, they pushed the mixed bunch of steers and a few cows toward the pens. The scene was a melee of dust and men and bawling cattle. The boys who'd been working the north *brasada* had hazed in their last bunch too; all the branding traps were in use. As soon as he'd heard of these newfangled devices, Perry had had them installed in each hunt pen. He'd never seen one before nor had anyone on the crew, but those Perry had had built to his own design were efficient as hell. You could roadbrand the biggest and wildest cows with a third of the trouble and time it had taken to mark them by the old rope and throw method.

They ran their bunch through the gates of a half-filled pen and then watched a group of *vaqueros* haze in some unsuspecting cattle by crooning a brush lullaby. They pushed the cattle up to an isolated empty pen and funneled them expertly through the gate. Two riders sprang down and lifted the heavy poles into place and thonged them down while the wild ones, realizing the trap, milled helplessly around the enclosure.

Jed grinned, thinking of Perry's impatience with the Mexicans' unhurried method of cattle-catching. Nevertheless he'd had the good sense not to interfere with their traditional ways.

Perry was over by another pen, looking on as three hands spayed a young heifer. Jed rode over to him, halted and stepped down. He watched the "priding" of the heifer with interest. Controlled stockbreeding had been completely unknown in South Texas until a traveling man Perry had talked to in Moratown had mentioned seeing it done; Perry had promptly pressed him for all the details.

Now every heifer with bad conformations was herded into a branding trap and caught in the squeeze by the head and front quarters. Her hindquarters were twisted down till her left flank was uppermost, a small cut made with a sharp knife high on her right flank. A stick with a chain loop tied at the end was inserted and twisted to foul the "pride" or ovaries. This was pulled out, the incision sewed up and a back of hot grease plastered over it to seal out flies and screwworms. Perry had also ordered all inferior bulls to be shot for table beef or else sent to the hide and tallow plants.

Perry slapped Jed on the shoulder. "What do you think of that? Give me a few years and all the wild and inferior chaff will be winnowed out. We'll have the best damned stocker herds in the country."

The men finished packing grease on the heifer's flank. Bull Jack and the other puncher holding down her hindquarters released her and the terrified animal lunged up. The other men got efficiently out of the way as she bolted free of the trap, but her shoulder slammed Bull Jack and knocked him sprawling. One of the punchers laughed.

Bull Jack climbed to his feet, red with fury. "I'll kill that goddam cow," he snarled.

Perry sauntered forward. "All you're going to do is fork another one in there and do it right. You do anything else and I'll kick your tail so high you'll be crying out your asshole."

The thickset man blinked and glared. He wiped a thumb across his dusty jaw, then moved heavily back to his job. The other punchers exchanged glances. They could understand a reprimand but not a rough-mouthing of that sort. Perry knew how to slip the needle to a man with cold accuracy, but as often as not he did it with a wrong-headed malice that was conscious of itself and didn't give a damn.

He glanced at Jed. "Let's get some coffee."

They walked over to a *carreta* pulled up by the spring. It was loaded with utensils. Soogans and other plunder were strewn around under the cottonwoods. Perry had a half-dozen men remain camped by the pens every night against any possible contingency. If those gates got opened some night, the whole gather might be scattered from hell to breakfast by morning. Perry and Jed got two cups from the *carreta* and walked to the fire where a big cowcamp coffeepot was bubbling. They filled their cups and sat on their haunches, swigging the Triple X black and hot.

"That's the fourth time," Jed said idly.

"What?"

"Fourth time I've seen you tear Bull Jack down in front of the others."

"Been keeping count, have you? He's an insolent bastard. I'll bust it out of him or I'll bust him out of here."

Perry's voice had an edge. He flicked the dregs of his coffee into the fire and stared narrow-eyed at Aaron Troop as he tramped toward them from the pens. That was another thing, Jed thought. The way Perry had been pushing the range boss. Pushing—no other word for it. The days weren't long enough for Troop to crowd in all the tasks assigned him. Petty grinding busywork, most of it.

Troop was tough as hell, but the grind was starting to show. His clothes were caked with dust; his eyes were red-rimmed, his walk stiff with exhaustion. He came up batting his dusty hat against his chaps.

"You got about as much as you can handle with a twenty-man trail crew," he observed. "When do they go up the trail?"

"Three days should be enough to finish the branding and 'priding.' You'll take 'em up yourself."

Troop's eyes flickered coldly; he nodded and walked away. Odd devil, Jed thought. No man of his crew would have taken the driving he had taken and stayed on, and Troop was tougher than any of them. Yet never a murmur of complaint from him. Jed wondered if Perry were trying to break him because of Troop's feeling for Elizabeth. And if Elizabeth were Troop's sole reason for staying on . . .

"We have a visitor," Perry murmured.

A rider was coming down on the flats out of the south. Even from here you could tell it was a woman, sidesaddle, her black skirt furling up a little in the wind. Perry stood up and walked to the south end of the spring and stood waiting, hands on his hips. Jed finished his coffee and followed him.

She was riding toward the pens. It was Elena Parral, Jed saw, and now she saw the Starbucks and veered over to them and halted her black Arabian. Jed pulled off his hat. Perry left his on, giving her a hard quizzical smile. Elena's glance touched from him to Jed.

"Hello." Her voice was neither friendly nor unfriendly.

"Hello," said Jed.

"Any business you have here," Perry said amiably, "you can take up with me. Otherwise you can turn right around and hightail the hell out of here, Miss Parral."

She might have stiffened a little, otherwise her poise and expression didn't change. She was dressed in mourning black, boots to porkpie hat, except for a white silk scarf at her throat. Her features were indistinct through a wisp of black veil.

"I ought to," she said quietly, "but I think

my pride can survive your insults till I've said what I came to. It's important enough to warrant that."

"Must be, for you to get let out alone. I thought spicks kept a close rein on their women."

"You can be sure my brother doesn't know I am here. Are you aware, Mr. Starbuck, that it is probable he'll never walk again? That his face is so hideously scarred his closest friends would no longer recognize him?"

"Well, Miss Parral, that's life. It marks us all, sho nuff." Perry folded his arms. "You have one minute to kindly tell me what the hell you're doing here."

Jed said flatly: "Perr!" And waited till Perry glanced at him. "Don't talk that way to her again."

"What if I do?"

Jed didn't reply, just watched him. He knew Perry could whip him, but he also knew he could last out a stand-up fight far better than he could have a few months ago.

Perry laughed and shook his head. "Jesus," he said. "All right." He swept off his hat, bowing. "Ma'am, do forgive the rough edges on an ole country boy from the barbarous north, as your late father had it."

"Why do you do what you've done?" she said quietly. "If it's for what my brother did to you . . ."

"No, that score's paid. Let me lay it out for you. I consider the strip north of the Mora open range." Perry ran a finger over his scarred cheek. "I paid my dues. You want to work that strip, go ahead, so will I. You leave my branded critters alone, I leave yours alone."

"You think my brother will accept that?"

"You tell me."

"That is why I came. He means to serve you a lesson, he says. Tonight our men will come to your pens. They will come suddenly and by surprise. By morning there will be many dead cattle in the pens."

"Well, well." Perry nudged his hat off his forehead. "He tell you that?"

"I overheard him tell Tito Rozales. He gave Tito the order. Tito did not like it, but Augustin is now the *patrón*. Tito will do what the head of the Parral family tells him to do, as his father and grandfather did before him. It was Tito who talked Augustin out of striking back when our father was killed. But now you've come on Parral land which Tito's family and their relatives have defended for us a hundred years. With the Hobarts, we made agreements. But you did not ask, you came and took."

"All right, bright lady, he's your brother. Suppose I'd asked, would it make any difference?"

"You know it wouldn't," she said evenly. "Augustin hates you. If he could destroy you in one stroke, he would. Tito persuaded him that to try would be foolish, it would only bleed both sides dry. But now you've given him the excuse, he will hurt you if he can, he will risk a war."

Perry's hard stare slanted up at her. "You're a Parral and you came to warn me. Why?"

"My father is dead, my brother crippled for life. *Santa Maria!* isn't that reason enough to avoid more—and worse? You can do this, you can move your cattle out of here. Today. Start your drive. When the *vaqueros* come, they will find empty pens, there will be no fight."

"You've been out in the sun a mite long, señorita. Or you take me for a damned fool. Which is it?"

"You are a fool," she said bitterly. "I know my brother is a fool. I came hoping against all appearances that you were not, that you can be reasoned with. If you avoid a fight now and stay off the Parral grant in the future, it is not too late, there can still be peace."

Perry rubbed his chin and glanced at Jed. "That might make sense."

"You know it does," Jed said evenly.

"Well, I'm not sure. Her brother is a headstrong lad."

"He doesn't listen to me," Elena said. "If he did, I could tell him that you would honor the Parral grant. But it would do no good and so he will raid your pens and then you will strike back some way, isn't that so?"

"Yes, indeed," Starbuck smiled. "I guess it wouldn't hurt to try it your way, move the cattle out today. *Mil gracias.*"

"I did nothing for you."

She nodded to led, touched the Arabian's flank with her crop and he moved off at a brisk trot. Jed followed her with his eyes till he heard Perry laugh quietly. "A proud and tempered little filly, that. But a chucklehead too."

Jed eyed him narrowly. "What've you got in mind?"

"Something like a surprise for old friend Augustin. He wants to serve me a lesson so damned bad. I think tonight we'll serve him one."

The night wind was almost cold. Jed hadn't particularly noticed it till he began to sweat with the waiting and then he felt it sharp on his skin and through his clothes. A cramp grabbed him across the shoulders, and he rocked on his heels, trying to ease it. But they had orders to keep quiet and not move around, so you couldn't loosen your muscles or slap yourself for warmth. You stayed crouched in the brush, rifle across your knees, and just waited.

At his elbow, Poke Tanner whispered: "Cold, ain't it?"

"Yeah."

Jed let his gaze range across the open splashes of ground and the masses of black brush where other men were laid up in pairs too, crouched and waiting. It was nearly midnight, he guessed, the darkness total except for the quarter moon's misty glow. Perry had chosen each position himself and had chosen well. Assuming the raiders would come straight up from the south, they'd pass across a roughly open avenue between mottes of brush and could be taken in a crossfire from both sides.

There was a glow of fires from the campsite by the spring. Everything had to look as usual to give the effect of a few men being on guard, a few sitting ducks who could be easily overpowered.

Finding that they'd ridden into a flap, would the Parral men give up? No way of being sure. Jed had argued with Perry—why not follow Elena Parral's suggestion? As lief try to budge a mountain. Perry had an answer to everything. Who was making a raid on who? Parral men were coming on his land to kill his cattle. Trespasser looking to destroy your property had to be impressed with the consequences of his action to head off any future ones. They'd be given a chance to surrender, more than they deserved. Perry didn't consider that he'd given the Parral girl any solid promise and besides he didn't trust her. She was a Parral, that was reason enough.

Jed rubbed a hand up and down the barrel of his Springfield. If he had to use it, what would he do? The horses? No, not that. Wing a man or two? Face to face with the choices, he felt a wave of revulsion. If he weren't ready to make a fight, what business did he have being here? If he were sure the thing was necessary . . .

He picked up a rustle of hoofs before he

saw the riders. They were below the silhouette of a rise, not skylined, but pretty soon the hazy moonlight showed them coming in a strungout line. They compressed to a long file as they funneled into the brush- free lane and rode straight toward the pens. The sandy ground muffled their approach. All was quiet except for the soft chink of spurs and bit chains and the faint stirrings of penned cattle.

Now the riders were jogging past the low clots of brush where the TH riders were laid up.

"Give up!" Perry's sudden roar from somewhere to Jed's left. "Throw down your guns!"

On the instant, somebody fired. The shot might have come from either side—no telling. Now a blaze of gunfire sputtered from both flanks. A horse screamed and went down. Jed saw two saddles suddenly emptied. Pandemonium. The Parral men yelling and firing blindly. Tito Rozales's bull voice roaring for them to retreat. But they were milling aimlessly, thrown into complete confusion by the slashing fire of an enemy they couldn't see.

Jed fired his Springfield once, shooting over their heads. He guessed that quite a few of TH's half-Mexican crew were doing the same.

As prearranged, the TH men began pouring out of the brush at either end of the open area, closing off escape. Then Perry was yelling over and over, "Hold your fire! Hold your fire!"

The command was directed at both sides. It had a quick effect, as if nobody had any heart for fighting. The shooting slacked off and it was over. Finished in a minute or less.

"Rozales," Perry shouted, "tell your men to throw down their guns. Throw 'em down or by God we'll cut you to pieces!"

Tito Rozales gave the order in quick Spanish. He made a thick anonymous shape on horseback, riding down the line of his men and repeating the order. A curse and a hard cuffing blow as he forced one reluctant *vaquero* to obey. Then he called, *"Está bien . . .* we are yours."

"Just stay like you are," Perry said.

A stink of burned powder singed the air pungent as garlic. Perry came striding into the open, rapid-firing orders. One TH man fetched a chunk of fire; two others heaped up a pyre of brush. When the fire had been built up, washing in oily flickers across the line of disarmed *vaqueros,* Perry ordered their guns gathered up.

"All of you step down," he said. "Off your horses. Tell 'em, Rozales."

Slowly and sullenly the *vaqueros* obeyed. At least seven of them were favoring wounds, slight or serious. Two were groaning on the ground, two more lay still and twisted in the positions they'd fallen. One horse was dead, another down and thrashing around, its head lifting and thudding down on the earth again and again.

Perry ordered his men to come out and keep the Parral men covered. As they emerged from the brush, Perry took a headcount. No casualties, a few minor wounds. One man sat on the ground and cursed as he worked off his boot, blood gouting from his knotty calf. Perry ordered the dying horse to be finished off. He glanced at Jed, who had moved up beside him.

"You're the big thinker," he said harshly. "Was I wrong?"

"I don't know," Jed said quietly. "But you do, don't you? You're never wrong."

Perry laughed.

Tito Rozales examined the two dead *vaqueros.* Speaking quietly, he assigned several of his men to look after those who were injured. He stared at Perry then, his chin grooving deep into its wreath of brown jowls.

"You are a cold-blooded *bastardo,* eh?"

Perry walked up to him and halted less than two feet from him. "You have it right, Porky. Don't like it when it kicks back, do you?"

"Look at them, gringo. Two dead men."

"They bought in. They knew what they were doing. So did you. You just got luckier, Porky."

"You are still what I say."

"You weren't coming to pay my cows a sociable visit. And if my few men you'd expected to find had got in your way, that'd be too damned bad, wouldn't it? A Comanche could take some tricks from you boys. So you watch your big lip. I don't think I can swallow very much shit about Christian conduct from you."

Tito's heavy mouth twisted. *"Qué lastima.* What do you do now?"

Perry glanced at the two men standing by the fire. "Fetch more brush. I want that fire built up till you can't get inside ten feet of it." He looked at Rozales. "You're going to do it. You're going to strip your horses of saddles and bridles. You're going to take

177

your boots off. Then you're going to walk by that fire one at a time and you're going to throw those saddles and bridles and boots into it. We'll take care of your horses. With a running start, they should make it home before you do."

"These dead. These wounded. Do they walk too?"

"If they can walk. You get home, send back for the rest. A wagon. Don't send anything else."

Tito shrugged. *"Le toca jugar,"* he murmured.

"Eso es, Porky. It's my turn to play. Something else too. You tell that busted-up wolf you work for he had better leave it where it is. Whole lot of things he can do if he wants. Shoot my stock. Run it off. He can hire *pistoleros,* eh?" Perry paused. "You tell him I can match him gun for gun, bullet for bullet. I can do any thing on his range he can do on mine. Any damned little thing. You tell him any time he thinks it's worth cutting his dogs loose, just go ahead, all right?"

Chapter 12

Elena stood in her camisole before her tall Adamesque mirror, frowning at her slight figure. She would never have to worry about becoming overdeveloped, that was certain. Luckily she had a pert heart-shaped face that men found interesting. Also a dainty smallness of limb and the long well-shaped legs of a horsewoman—as well as one could develop such on a side-saddle. But hardly appreciable assets in the heavy voluminous dresses of her station, particularly the stiff black taffetas she'd worn of late.

The mirror reflected her bed where the maid was laying out her costume for the day, Impulsively Elena said: "Chavela, I want something bright today. A gingham, I think. The plaid will do nicely—"

The whisper of Chavela's rope-soled sandals halted between commode and closet; her heavy-browed reflection showed disapproval. "You will come out of mourning so soon, señorita?"

"Yes." Elena's tone indicated that the matter wasn't open to discussion. "And tell

Rufio that I will have my breakfast in the patio . . ."

A half-hour later she came out to the open stone-walled square set off behind the great rambling Parral *hacienda*. Morning sun drenched the walls and flagstones; she felt pretty and pleasant in her crisp plaid and the cheery ribbon that circled the tight bun of her blue-black hair. She seated herself at a heavy trestle table under a *ramada* and savored the morning while Rufio, the ancient houseservant, brought her breakfast tray. Elena smiled a little to herself. No doubt Augustin would be furious when he learned of her early emergence from mourning. But then he'd always railed at many of her habits and preferences, from the rides she liked to take alone to her bacon-and-egg Anglo-style breakfasts.

Sipping coffee from a thin china cup, she gazed at the scarred old walls that surrounded the patio, walls deeply notched to provide firing positions for defense of the *hacienda*. She barely remembered the only time these had seen use: an attack by howling Comanches when she was six. A memory savagely vivid enough to sober her thoughts to the trouble that loomed so near these days.

She did not wonder too much about whether she'd done the right thing in warning the Starbucks of the impending raid. Positiveness had always been one of her virtues (if such were ever a virtue in a woman, she thought wryly). It hadn't been a question, after all, of betraying her own. Merely one of seeing that senseless bloodshed was avoided. Perry Starbuck had agreed to move his cattle out as she'd suggested, so she had done the sensible thing.

"Señorita." Rufio spoke softly as, emerging from the *hacienda* he respectfully halted a few feet from her table. "The *patrón* asks that you come to his room."

"When I have finished coffee. Kindly tell the *patrón.*"

The old servant bowed slightly and shuffled back into the house. Elena refilled her cup, enjoying the freedom she'd lately felt to speak and do much as she pleased. Yet it was sad and embittering that the hopeless crippling of her brother had made such freedom possible.

Ugly times had fallen on the Parrals. On the home she loved. In a single day of violence, her father had been killed, Augustin permanently crippled. Everything touching her life had been changed. Laughter had

181

gone out of the *hacienda,* the servants tip-toed about their tasks. The only voice that one ever heard raised these days was Augustin's, storming in one of his black furies at something or someone.

Finishing her coffee, Elena rose and walked into a cool and shadowed hall where bedchambers branched off. As she neared Augustin's door, something crashed against it and Augustin shouted: "Get out, you son of a sow! Get out or I'll see your bastardly hide stretched on a curing frame!"

The door was flung open and Rufio scurried out, his seamed face pinched with fright. He saw Elena and came to a stop.

"What is it, Rufio?"

"He said his coffee was cold, Señorita," the old man husked. "He threw the tray at my head.'"

"Go on, Rufio. I'll speak with him."

She walked to the door and halted at the threshold, looking down at a litter of utensils and food that had been Augustin's breakfast. Stepping around the splash of coffee soaking into a striped blanket-rug, she approached his wheelchair.

"You wanted to see me?" she asked calmly.

"Ten minutes ago," he snarled, "yes!"

The room was in semidarkness, for the

windows were covered by heavy-weave blankets through which light barely filtered. Augustin insisted on this condition whenever it was necessary for others to see him, but the muted gloom wasn't sufficient to hide the terrible mutilation of his face. What had been livid lacerations were fading to scars like pale worms. A particularly gruesome one at the corner of his mouth had warped its silky hint of cruelty to a perpetual grimace. His broken left arm had healed badly; the elbow projected at a stiff crook. A blanket covered his legs—the legs he still tried every day with the aid of crutches, always raging and incredulous when not a muscle would function. A savage poetic justice, for Augustin had crippled more than one good horse during his tantrum-wild binges. But a justice which had scatter-fired on those around him, as pain and brooding turned him totally vicious.

"Come here," he said imperatively.

Elena came close to the wheelchair. His hand leaped out and seized her wrist.

"Now," he whispered, "we shall have the truth. Yesterday Tito and I spoke together in this room. I think you heard us." His hand tightened and savagely twisted, forcing her down on her knees. Pain convulsed her arm and shoulder; she cried out. "Did you? Speak up!"

"Yes! Yes, I did—"

"Did you go to that man Starbuck and tell him what you heard?"

"Yes!"

He cursed and flung her away. Elena fell heavily to the rug, then got slowly to her feet. Watching her brother's face. Shocked at the hatred that blazed there.

"I thought that was it," he hissed. "How else could it have been? The hostler told Tito you went for a long ride yesterday. That man Starbuck is my enemy and you betrayed us to him."

She stood rubbing her wrist, staring at him defiantly. "And if I did?"

"Because you did, two of our men were killed last night."

Elena was shaken; she swallowed hard. "Killed . . . ?"

"Yes, my dear sister. Killed. Because your meddling allowed Starbuck to lay an ambush for our men. Was that also your advice?"

"No," she whispered. "I told him to move out his cattle at once. To avoid killing."

"Ah. To avoid it." His laugh was harsh and jarring. "How do you feel now, 'Lena?"

"How did *you* feel?" Her hands clenched at her sides. "When you decided to slaughter TH's cattle, did you care if men guarding the pens were killed? *Dios!* You dare to judge my action?"

"Of course not," he said mockingly. "I only wished you to know. You're abundantly possessed, my dear 'Lena, of that most useless of all human encumbrances. A conscience."

"Which you are not and have never been."

"Exactly. On your way out, kindly tell that ancient mutt Rufio to come here and help me onto my crutches. I have a feeling that I'll be free of this accursed chair before long."

"You'll never be!" In the heat of her anger, Elena let the words spill out unheedingly. "Don't you know that yet? You'll never walk again!"

His eyes narrowed to slits. "Walk? Of course I will," he said softly. "Why shouldn't I? When my back is healed . . ."

Elena swallowed, sensing the enormity of what her words may have triggered. For in the back of his mind, she was sure, Augustin knew the truth he wouldn't admit. But sooner or later it must be flatly stated. Why not now?

He must have read some of this in her face.

"You lie," he spat. "The doctor said there was no telling yet."

"He said six weeks. It has been six weeks and more, Augustin. There can no longer be doubt. The spine will not heal . . . you will not walk again."

"You lie!" he shouted. "You lying treacherous witch—"

His hands spun the chair wheels, propelling him toward her. Elena retreated swiftly to the doorway. His face was contorted, the wormlike scars twisting.

"Get out!" he screamed. "Leave here! Leave this house! Take everything you have and get out!"

Elena ran to her room and bolted the door behind her. Suddenly she was afraid. Did he mean it? She flung herself on the bed, pressing her face to the pillow. She lay quietly, heart pounding, listening to the small noises of the house.

Spurs chinked on the stone floor of the hall. Someone tapped softly on the door. "Señorita?"

Recognizing the voice, she went quickly to the door, shot back the bolt and opened it. Tito Rozales stood there, hat in hand. His brown sweating face glistened; he looked supremely uncomfortable.

"The *patrón* says you are to pack your belongings," he said. "If you are slow about it, I am to tell my wife Chavela to help you. Then you are to be taken to the ranch of Arturo Mariel."

Elena met his eyes levelly. "I am Don Solano's daughter. Have you forgotten?"

"No, señorita. I do not forget. I have watched over you and Don Augustin all your lives; I have feelings for both. But your brother is *patrón* now and he is the one we must obey. It has always been so." A strain entered Tito's voice. "It is hard enough for me to do. I ask you not to make it harder."

The Mariels. Poor but respected distant cousins of the Parrals. Arturo and his wife Lupe would warmly welcome her, Elena knew; her fate could be far worse. She masked her thoughts with a stiff-faced pride.

"Do as you will," she said. "If you'll hitch up a wagon, I will be ready shortly . . ."

The ham and eggs were marbled with grease and the coffee was tepid, and Jed wasn't particularly hungry anyway. But he tackled the cold breakfast with a false appetite, knowing that if it went down leadenly now, he'd be glad enough later in the day that he'd filled up. Both he and Perry had overslept after last night's long vigil at the pens. Now they occupied themselves with a cheerless breakfast while Elizabeth gave them a piece of her mind.

"Are you *trying* to tear down all that my father built up? What he died to hold intact? Is that it, Perry?"

Perry looked up from his plate, annoyed. "I've been over all that with you. If you're not convinced of my side, then at least don't interfere with me."

Elizabeth was sitting tensely upright, palms flat on the table. She stared at him in outrage. "Don't *interfere?* Are you forgetting who owns this place?"

Perry rested a pointed look on her. "You can start giving the orders any time," he said softly. "Just remember that the day you start, I am packing out of here and leaving you to whistle *Dixie.* And if I ever do leave, it'll be for good."

"I—I don't want you to leave. I just . . ."

"Yes?" His tone turned faintly jeering. "You what, Beth?"

Which touched a fresh nerve of anger. "I am just wondering," she said icily, "what it will take to satisfy you, Perry. Now it's only

188

to work the brush of the Mora strip. So you say. Yet last night you laid an ambush that resulted in killing."

"Listen, I told you. Parral named the turn. I called him, that's all. If I hadn't, he'd tromp all over us."

"But two men died! If you hadn't gone into the Mora in the first place . . . What will it be next? How far will you go?"

Perry laughed and swiped a napkin across his mouth, then scraped back his chair and stood. "Stop worrying. Jesus, honey, I told you—men are men. Life's a rough game and if you lose, you pay what you've staked. Your life too, come to that." He kissed the side of her neck and patted her shoulder. "Finish your coffee, kid, and let's rustle it."

He tramped out of the house.

Elizabeth sat bitter-eyed, her spread fingers shaping into fists. "I'm glad Pa can't know how costly his Samaritan gesture would prove to be. But that's not right, is it? I made the real choice . . . I married the man."

Jed gazed at her across the rim of his cup, troubled. "You're just upset, Beth. You have to make allowances."

"The way you do? You're damned right I'm upset!"

"It's not a matter of approving everything he does," Jed argued. "It's a matter of loyalty. I'm his brother, you're his wife. That should count for something."

"Oh God, don't tell me about feelings." She dropped her face against one hand, shaking her head. "Don't you see that's all of it? Feelings—do you think I'd care half as much if I didn't love him so? He's becoming more coarse, more intense, more driving. Surely you've seen that!"

"Yeh," Jed muttered.

"Then you're concerned too; I know it. Jed, I don't just mean for the events he's setting in motion, alarming as that may be. I mean for what it's doing to him."

Jed gazed glumly into his cup. It was true. Now that Perry had power to play with, the uses of it intrigued him much as a fragile, complex, and even dangerous toy might fascinate a precocious child. But was that reason enough to repudiate him? Perry might have been right in taking the action he had last night. Anyway, Jed thought, it was best he stick fast and hope that his presence would provide something of a braking force on Perry. Not, he thought bleakly, that he'd ever had much effect that way. Any more than Elizabeth seemed to be having . . .

Jed finished his coffee and headed for the corral where, as always, the crew had assembled to receive the day's orders. Some sort of altercation was brewing as Jed came up. He wasn't surprised to see that the adversaries were Perry and Bull Jack. They were facing each other beside the corral gate and the crew was pulling off from them now. Perry stood hipshot and relaxed. Bull Jack's stance was belligerent; he fisted a half-coiled rope in one paw.

"I taken all the rawhiding from you I'm gonna!" he bellowed.

"Then pack your plunder," Perry said curtly. "Pack it now and get out."

Sidling up by Poke Tanner, Jed said softly: "What happened?"

"Jack was trying to throw his hull on one o' his string," Poke murmured. "Hoss shied and bumped him. 'Stead o' cheeking him, Jack larruped him across the eyes with his rope. Perry give his ole ass a good blistering."

"You don't give me no more orders," Bull Jack snarled, "and I ain't leaving without I hear the Major's daughter say so."

"You're leaving now. On your feet or on your belly. Take your choice."

A mad-dog light quivered in Bull Jack's

eyes. "You move me, you goddam Yankee-fied bastard."

Unhesitatingly Perry started for him, flinging up an arm to strike aside the coiled rope as Bull Jack swung it at his head. His doubled fist sank into the bulky man's kettle gut. Bull Jack grunted heavily but didn't fall back by a step. Perry's other hand chopped against his face and then Perry was moving back and away from him like fluid lightning. Bull Jack stood there with his nose dissolved to a fleshy pulp, rivulets of blood streaming down either side of his mouth.

He blinked tearfully. Then roared *"Goddam!"* And lunged at Perry with a wild swing that failed to connect. Perry was already weaving sideways and past him, hammering him savagely in the kidneys. When Bull Jack spun to face him, Perry's fist cracked against his bullet brow, splitting the skin. Bull Jack pulled back several steps now, pawing blindly at the blood running into his eyes.

Perry stalked him at a ferocious half-lope and hit him again. Bull Jack slammed against the corral poles and bounced off them. Perry caught him with a stiff hook that snapped his head back. He followed this with a full minute of brutal punishment. Cutting Bull Jack down with a methodical and merciless zeal, beating him to a bloody wreck, finally looping an underhand right to his jaw that dropped him on his face.

Perry looked at his raised fists. They were smeared with blood, none of it his own. He let his hands fall to his sides and said: "Throw some water on him. Soon as he can stand, set him on a horse and point him away from here."

Someone dipped a bucket of water from the horsetrough an poured it over Bull Jack. Groaning, he heaved over on his back, but made no effort to get up. His face was slashed bloody raw and it was obvious he wouldn't be able to sit a horse for a while.

The crew turned away, some silent, some muttering. Perry had done himself no good in their eyes, that was sure. The fight had been his all the way, yet he'd gone savagely beyond necessity in punishing the recalcitrant crewman. That was the thing Jed would remember most . . .

Chapter 13

The trail drives to Abilene met with little success in this year of 1867. A depression had struck the East. Newspapers reported long queues of the unemployed being fed at the Tombs in New York City, but the food wasn't beef or even beef broth. Though the demand for beef was greater than ever, practically nobody had the money to buy it. A shrunken market had many cattlemen declaring a decision to make no drive at all this year.

Leandro Mirabel and Rubio Perez, bossing the first two TH herds sent north, ran into considerable trouble. Heavy rains mired the Chisholm Trail; swollen rivers made for dangerous crossings. Choctaw renegades struck at their herds in the Nations; in Kansas they were raided more than once by the off-scourings of wartime guerrilla bands. A cholera epidemic which had begun among soldiers assigned to guard the Kansas Pacific tracklayers had spread across Kansas like wildfire, even hitting the drovers on trail.

Leandro and Rufio's herds were stalled for several weeks by the contagion. When they did reach Abilene, it was to learn that the first drovers to arrive had sold their herds at good prices in the tight and limited market. But once the first trainloads of longhorns had reached Chicago and the depressed East, prices had plummeted. At this point Leandro and Rubio were lucky to break even. While Aaron Troop, arriving nearly a month later, found no market at all. He managed to dispose of his herd at a slight loss to a U. S. Indian agent who had to fill a beef ration for his reservation wards.

The skimpy returns that the returning trail bosses were able to report came as a blow to Perry. His driving and impulsive nature had made him gamble too much: he'd hatched grandiose plans which he would be unable to implement.

He began to drink more, and when he drank he became morose and ugly. But the brooding change in him went deeper, Jed realized. Not that the misfortune with the herds had slackened the reckless intensity of his ambitions. It had merely transformed them from zesty enthusiasms to taut obsessions.

Perry had always driven himself fiercely; that didn't change. But now his violent energies seemed to seek a different focus. He spent more and more time away from home. On business speculations, he said. But he declined to discuss his activities with Jed or Elizabeth, and Jed found something sullen and furtive in his evasions. A hint of bloat began to tinge his big frame, the unhealthy flesh of excessive drinking. And he'd become increasingly insensitive to the opinions of others.

Jed was present one day when Perry beat up and fired a crewman named Perth for maltreating a horse. It was even more savage than his retribution on Bull Jack for a similar reason. Perry went after the man with a cruel fury which convinced Jed that Perth's real offense hadn't been to brutalize a horse; it had been to offend Perry. He noticed something else too: that Perry was able to beat the slight, wiry Perth less easily than he had the powerful Bull Jack. And that it left him slightly fatigued.

Shortly afterward five of the crew quit in a body. "We taken enough of that mean-tempered bastard's ways," said one. Perry returned from his next trip with a half-dozen new hands. But there was a difference about these men And more of the crew quietly packed their warbags, collected their pay and left TH . . .

When Elena had said she was going for a ride today, Arturo had immediately wanted to know where she intended to ride. She was frank enough: she had not seen her friend Elizabeth at the TH ranch in a long while, since before her marriage, and she wanted to visit her.

Arturo had shaken his head as if he disapproved. He did not say so directly, but his square-set face with its great looping mustaches was very serious. "You will be careful then, Cousin. The man Starbuck is your brother's enemy."

"Yes, Augustin made that clear enough. Don't worry."

"Get an early start back." Arturo had peered at the sky. "There will be rain before dark, I think."

Elena smiled now as she rode straight east toward the TH headquarters. With seven children to look after and a workday that kept them toiling from dawn to dusk, Arturo and Lupe still found time to be concerned for her, their rich cousin. They'd rarely thought of her as such, for she had seen them often since she was a small girl. She'd always looked forward to her visits to their little ranch, poor in goods and rich in love and laughter. There'd been little of that in the Parral *hacienda* except, until recently, among the servants.

She was surprised at how little she missed the great house and its palatial appointments and being waited on in the stiff splendor that she had been raised to believe was a Parral's due. Plain meals and hard work were her lot with the Mariels; she had refused to accept the half-deferential manner that the older children had been inclined to show her at first. They liked her, but they had been awed, too, that one of the rich cousins had come to live with them. She had quickly overcome that by pitching in with a will, but it was good to finally get away on one of the lonely rides she had always loved so well.

Star tossed his head and she reined him down with a brisk, no-nonsense hand, then patted his neck. She had not expected to see her favorite horse again; she'd been pleased as a child when Tito Rozales had shown up at the Mariels' a week ago, leading the thoroughbred. Was this a gift from her brother, she had wondered, hoping Augustin might be having a change of heart. No, Tito had shaken his heavy head, the *patrón* did not know of this, but as he never went near the stables any more, he would never learn of it. Chavela and the other servants would never tell him. The horse was truly hers and Tito Rozales had brought him to her . . .

Elena had nearly cried. She still had friends at the *hacienda*, friends who would not forget her. Thinking of it helped her to enjoy this ride, alone with her thoughts, across the shaggy sedgegrass prairie with its isolated groves of oak and pecan and its ancient buffalo wallows, dried up now in the late summer heat but soon to offer a winter haven for thousands of wild ducks and curlews and whooping cranes from Canada and the Dakotas. It was a world Elena had always known and she was comfortable in it. Though not in the decorous black riding costume that had been her mother's; she always felt like a prisoner in the heavy confinement of its brocaded pleats and folds.

She crossed a creek and pushed her mount through a clogging straggle of mesquite and thorny brazil brush, and then crossed a shallow rise. Below, in its long well-grassed trough of a valley, lay the TH headquarters. Elena put Star briskly down the slope and swung south around the outbuildings and the bunkhouse-cookshack with its covered runway. Several men were lounging there. Though she passed them by a good two hundred feet, she was aware of their crass stares and insulting remarks. She couldn't make out the words, but the tone was plain enough.

Her face burning, Elena rode on to the main house. She saw Elizabeth out in her little garden, shears in hand, snipping cuttings off her Prairie Queen rosebushes. "Beth!" she called. Elizabeth's sun-flushed face turned with a quick pleasure. She was wearing an old dress, her hair tied up in a faded scarf. " 'Lena . . . oh it's so good to see you."

Elena unshipped herself from the sidesaddle, careful to avoid hanging up her skirt which had lead sewn into the seam to keep it draped neatly down. She and Elizabeth embraced and Beth gave her a critical regard and said almost enviously: "You look very well, 'Lena."

"And very brown, no?" Elena laughed. "I suppose you've heard."

"That you were dispossessed . . . or evicted? Yes, word gets about; the Mexican people see to that. But hard work and sunshine certainly agree with you. You've put on a little weight. And very becomingly."

Elena drew off her gloves. "Beth, who are those men by the bunkhouse? Not regular hands, I'd say."

"No." Elizabeth's voice turned tight and hard. "You would have to call them what they are. Gunmen. Hardcases. Ne'er-do-wells. They were hired for one special talent and it is not to work."

"I see." Elena's brows drew together. "Beth, I should think he—your husband—has made all the point he needed to. I don't think my brother will risk any further retaliation. But just what does Perry Starbuck have in mind?"

"Oh Lord, don't ask me. I never know what he's going to do next." Vaguely she clipped off a rose cutting and laid it in the basket on her arm. "This soil is so dry. Too dry for Southern roses, I believe. My mother brought them from Virginia ages ago." She smiled brightly. "Shall we go inside and have a cup of tea?"

In the house, Elena took instant note of the stale taint of liquor and tobacco that hung in the rooms. No doubt Elizabeth and Ceferina kept other signs of a man's heavy drinking and smoking scrupulously cleared away, but the smells were ineradicable. Elizabeth chatted about inconsequential things as she set out the tea service. Elena felt the strain beneath, but said nothing. It was none of her affair unless Elizabeth chose to say something.

Elizabeth poured two cups full of steaming water. As she filled the second, her hand began to shake so that the teapot spout chattered against the cup rim. She set the pot down quickly and dropped onto the settee, covering her mouth with her hand.

"Oh 'Lena. Forgive me. I'm afraid it's nerves. It's . . . do you want to hear what it really is?"

"If you want to tell me."

"It's everything." Elizabeth's hands twisted whitely together on her lap. "His plans. All of his damned never-ending plans! He wants more land. And why, I ask him, do we need more land? Why, to build bigger and better herds. Do we need them? We're going to damned well have them. What if other land claimants object? Well, that's why we're hiring those gentlemen you saw by the bunkhouse. To take care of objections."

"Then *does* he plan more action against my brother?"

" 'Lena, honestly, I don't know. We can expand on our other sides, but will that satisfy him? I can't answer. I can't even talk with him any more. Try sparring at words with him and you'll come up piqued, smarting, holding the short end. He's become clever and secretive too. He goes on trips that last for days. When he comes home, all he does is drink and brood. I've no idea what he does or where he goes . . . except that the cheap perfume is the devil to wash out."

The acrid bitterness in her friend's voice shocked Elena. She didn't know what to say.

"He believes in nothing, 'Lena, he harbors no illusions whatever. It enables him to see through people like glass. Men and women alike. And he uses that talent to further his ends."

"And those . . . ?"

"God only knows. Greed—the play of power—the mere game of it. Perhaps all of them. I am never sure of anything with him. I thought that I could soften his headstrong ways. But I can't. When we're together, he—he sweeps me along with him." Elizabeth's voice dropped to a whisper. "I still love him, 'Lena. I—"

She stopped.

Someone had come in from the patio, tramping heavily through the house. Elizabeth made a plain effort at composing herself. In a moment Perry Starbuck appeared in the *sala* entrance, thrusting aside the beaded portieres. He halted, seeing them.

"What's she doing here?" His tone flicked her nerves like a blade.

"She is visiting. I have invited her in," Elizabeth said evenly. "Aren't you home rather soon? You've only been away two days."

Ignoring her, Starbuck walked to the sideboard and poured a drink. He downed it at once and poured another. Elena felt a faint repugnance. The man had subtly changed in the weeks since she'd last seen him. Or perhaps the change wasn't so subtle. Physically it was obvious enough. He didn't look fat—not at all but he was definitely heavier and he moved with a solid, thumping gait that seemed to dare anything to get in its way. He was unshaved, his broadcloth suit rumpled; his eyes were thicklidded and bloodshot.

He glanced at Elena and said almost impersonally, "I want her out of here," then swallowed his drink.

Elizabeth came to her feet, white-faced. "By what right do you—?"

"The one that says you honor and obey your husband. Remember it?" His face changed slightly; the set of his mouth seemed cruel. "I don't want any Parral setting foot on this place. Male or female. Is that clear enough?"

"She's staying, Perry! I've had enough of your bullying and your petty tyranny! Do you understand? I've had . . ."

Starbuck took three driving steps. He faced Elizabeth; his heavy hand cracked across her face. He turned and tramped to the *sala* entrance and paused, looking at Elena.

"Get out," he said flatly.

His footsteps echoed between walls; a door slammed behind him. Silence. Elizabeth stood fingering her cheek, the ivory skin showing prints of angry red. Tears glittered in her eyes.

"How often does that happen?"

"This was the first time. But you had better go, 'Lena. As you see, I can't even guarantee your safety here."

Elena stood up too. Again it was hard to find the right words. "Beth, if you should ever need . . . any sort of help, anything at all, send word to the Mariels."

"I will."

Elena went out through the patio. She untied her horse, mounted and waved goodbye to Elizabeth standing in the patio doorway, then heeled Star lightly around. Clouds were starting to mass darkly out of the west; she hoped she could reach the Mariel ranch before the storm hit. Wind coasting off the hills funneled eddies of dust across the ranchyard as she crossed it, this time swinging much wider of the outbuildings in order to avoid the bunkhouse entirely.

Ahead of her, a rider swung to sight, jogging toward the corrals. He saw Elena and turned his mount her way. The wind flapped his loose hatbrim up and down so that she didn't immediately identify him. Then he was close; she saw it was Jed Starbuck. He seemed bigger than she remembered, more imposing, she guessed because of the lean musculature that had broadened his chest and shoulders. He now held his saddle with a rangeman's solid presence. Elena was impressed and in the same instant decided not to show it.

"Afternoon." He touched his hat. "Were you visiting? I'm sorry I missed you."

"Are you," she said coolly. "Perhaps I should have visited your per cent of the ranch. Your brother doesn't want me on his. Or is it Beth's?"

"My per cent, eh? I guess nothing's a secret in this country." He smiled briefly. "So Perry's back. What did he say to you?"

"Nothing very interesting. Anyway I have to get home."

"May I ride part way with you?" Not waiting for an answer, Jed kneed his horse alongside hers. "I understand you're living with some cousins . . ."

"As you say, the country holds no secrets. Aren't you in from work early?"

He nodded thoughtfully. "I wanted to confer with Elizabeth . . . before Perry got back from his trip. Something's happened that'll mean trouble when he finds out. Serious trouble. I hoped that Beth and I might find a way to head him off. No chance of that now."

"What trouble?"

"Leandro Mirabel and I were ranging along Kenobee Creek this morning, making a range tally. We found carcasses of dead cattle all over the place. All of them shot."

"Do you think my brother ordered it done?"

"Do you?"

Elena bit her lip and shook her head. "I don't know. I can't deny what he's capable of. But killing off cattle on TH land . . . it seems like an empty goad that would merely invite trouble. I'd give Augustin credit for a bit more sense."

"It doesn't have to make sense to Perry. Hating your brother as he does, he's likely to guess the worst."

"He'll jump on any likely excuse, don't you mean?" A bitter disgust tinged her words. "They're very alike, your brother and mine. And deserving, I think, of whatever happens to them. The pity is that they'll drag the innocent with them."

"Perry has a code of his own," Jed said slowly. "In his own way, he lives by it. I don't say I agree with . . ."

"A code isn't enough," Elena said impatiently. "He does not feel, he can't. People are nothing to him. Except when he uses them."

"He doesn't use me."

"No? Then it's because in some selfish way he needs you. But he has surely used Beth."

"I think you're wrong," Jed said stubbornly. "He cares for her."

"You think," she said mockingly. "Well, my friend, I saw him slap her just now. Hard. What do you think of that?"

An angry light flickered in his glance, then died. He said tonelessly: "Why?"

"Does it matter? I felt like telling Beth to leave with me. But she wouldn't, I know." Elena hesitated, then added: "It's different with you. You can break with him any time. Get away from him. Why don't you?"

Jed scowled. "It doesn't work that way. You don't run out on somebody just because some of what he does rubs against the grain."

"Ah, that rings handsomely. If true. Or is it just that you lived too long in his shadow? That when all's said, you haven't a strength of your own?"

Jed reined his horse to a stop and hipped around, eying her levelly. "Is that what you think?"

"No," she said angrily. "I think you're worth ten of that man. Yet you go on finding excuses for him. And so for yourself—for staying by him. I hate to see it, that's all."

"Why?"

"Do you want to find out? Break with Perry Starbuck and then ask me." Almost furiously she twitched her rein to put Star forward, but immediately pulled up to look at him again. "You don't like the things he does. I don't think you even like him. You're only going through the motions—out of habit or loyalty, or whatever the reason. If you see that, Jed, and if you should want to tell me, you will know where to find me."

Chapter 14

As the evening wore on, the tension in the *sala* grew thick enough to cut with a knife. Perry had been drinking when Jed had returned from escorting Elena Parral part way to the Mariel ranch. He'd continued to steadily drink through supper, eating little, his mood temper-edged. Outwardly, at least, he might have been consuming so many shots of ice water for all that the liquor seemed to touch him. But Jed knew his brother, he knew that the booze would curdle like a black canker in Perry's gut and gradually inflame him.

It had been that way occasionally in the old days whenever a black mood had pushed him to drink. Now the moods were frequent and worse. So Jed was watchful. The dark shiny bruise on Elizabeth's jaw was reason enough for him not to retire early, though he was bone-tired from a long day. He sat on the sofa beside Elizabeth and watched Perry slowly pace the *sala,* halting from time to time at the sideboard to refill his glass. Christ, Jed thought, I've never seen him put it away like that. He'll fall on his face pretty soon . . .

But when Perry suddenly broke silence, his words were clear and unslurred. He wheeled on Elizabeth: "Goddammit, you can't let 'em get away with this!"

She was busy with crochet work, her lap filled with bright-colored Afghan squares, and she did not even look up. "I told you," she said in a calm even voice. "You may do whatever you like. But not with my ranch or my crew."

Perry violently flung out his arm, sloshing liquor from his glass as he pointed at the door. "Maybe I'll just call your damned bluff. Then we'll see!"

"Go ahead. Walk out the door. Ride as far away as you like. You'll not hold that over my head again, Perry. Whatever you do now, you'll do alone."

Perry swore and whirled, flinging his glass against a wall. It shattered to bits that rattled across the floor. Not looking up, Elizabeth called, "Ceferina!"

The housekeeper's broad frightened face poked through the portieres. "Señora?"

"Mr. Starbuck threw a glass at the wall. Will you get a broom, please, and sweep up the pieces?"

Ceferina withdrew hurriedly.

"Dammit, Beth . . ." Perry held out a shaking hand. "Someone slaughters your cattle, you don't just shrug it off! It's like handing 'em a license to pull more of the same—or worse—"

"I wouldn't really know, Perry. I do know that you are not going to use men of TH to make a retaliatory raid on the Parral place. Even if you knew that was done at Augustin's order—which you don't—there has been enough needless bloodshed. I mean to see there's no more. Not for this reason. Not for any reason."

Another silence gripped the room. Thunder rolled on the hills, shaking the house. Rain hissed and bounced on the roof. Perry stood tensely in the center of the room, legs spread, his face mottled with rage or drink. He was like a bull who'd run head-on into a stone wall and couldn't quite understand what had happened.

He had, quite simply, pushed Major Troy Hobart's daughter too far. He could soften her with love, he could talk her down, he could even mildly threaten her into acquiescence. But he couldn't knock her around like some saloon trollop and get away with it. Suddenly and stunningly, he'd been made aware of it.

Jed was pleased. But concerned, too, that Beth's courage might get her more of the same. Not while I'm here, he thought grimly. And he meant to stay where he was until Perry staggered to bed or passed out on his feet. Which appeared probable. He was starting to perceptibly sway on his feet now, the booze catching up with him in a rush. When he spoke again, his words were slushy and uncertain.

"You . . . goddamn . . . slut."

"Perry," Jed said, "shut your mouth and go to bed."

"What?"

Jed rose to his feet. "I said go to bed. Or I'll put you there."

Perry had trouble focusing his eyes. He barked a laugh. "Well how do you like that? Old Jed coming out mean. Thinks he can whip me."

"Right now," Jed said, "I can. Right now I could push you over with my little finger. Can you walk as far as your bed?"

Perry stared at him a long bleary moment. Laughed again. "Yeh," he muttered, "yeh," and turned with a heavy-footed care, starting for the portieres. He halted there and looked back at Jed and Elizabeth.

"You could both stand a shot of loyalty, by Christ. You—"

The shot was almost lost in a clarion peal of thunder. Two more shots crashed on the heels of it, merging with a crackle of shattering glass.

"Get down!" Jed yelled.

He dived for the candelabra on a lowboy,

swept it to the floor and threw his body across it to douse the flames. Night rushed into the room; so did rain and wind pouring through the broken window. Jed heard a crunch, of running feet outside, a sound that faded quickly.

He crawled to his feet.

"Perry!" Elizabeth cried. "Jed . . . ?"

"All right," Jed said. "Perr?"

"Yes, goddam it!" Perry's voice was sober, ragged, shaking. "What in hell was that?"

A jagged rope of lightning lit up the room. Elizabeth was still seated on the sofa, taut as a wire. Perry stood flattened to the wall, gripping one arm; his eyes stared wildly.

"Someone shot through the window," Jed said. Then he ran away. Maybe I can catch him."

As he spoke, he was crossing to the door, flinging it open and plunging out into the storm. It was at full fury, lashing silvery sprays of water against him. He stopped, squinting against the blinding gusts. Saw nothing till another flare of lightning picked out the dark form of a man running away from the house. He'd gone out the patio gate and was cutting toward the cottonwood grove to the east.

Jed started in that direction at a ground-eating lope.

Again lightning blazed, wiping away masses of shadow. He saw the man just ahead, pushing into the grove, and then heard a pounding of hoofs and a man's bull-chested curse. Another stroke of lightning showed a horse, riderless, streaking away from the trees. The assassin had left his mount tied here, and now, terrified by the thunder and intermittent flashes, it had broken away.

Jed lunged heedlessly into the grove, plowing his way through the undergrowth. He broke into a clearing and saw a dim form bulk suddenly ahead of him. Both men were in motion, unable to stop; they collided face-on. Hurt and dazed, Jed was aware of the ground slamming against his back. Blindly rolling on his side, he heard a close-by grunt that told him the enemy had fallen too, and now Jed clawed back the skirt of his coat.

He'd forgotten that he wasn't wearing his pistol.

An instant later he heard a gun hammer make a futile click not two feet away: the pin falling on a defective shell or cap. Two more clicks. The enemy's savage curse. Again the sound of feet running as he crashed away out of the grove.

Half-stunned, Jed lay where he was a few moments more. Staggering to his feet, he moved after the retreating sounds. Coming out of the trees, he heard the sloshing steps drift toward his right. Toward the outbuildings. Either the fellow was running blind or he was possessed by a panicked thought of losing himself among the sheds. If so, it was short-range thinking. The sheds would hide him temporarily, but he'd be quickly hunted down . . .

The shots had alerted the crew. Lamplight blazed in the windows and open doorway of the bunkhouse as the men spilled out into the storm to see what was going on. Their voices mingled loudly in the pelting rain. Cords of lightning rippling from sky to ground, washing the buildings into sudden relief, showed Jed the enemy's form as he disappeared behind a hayshed.

Hauling up now, Jed wiped a wet sleeve across his face. Help . . . he would need help. He tramped across the yard toward the crew's voices and their slicker-gleaming shapes. One of them spotted him and yelled a question. He replied, identifying himself.

A moment later the men had pulled

around him, and Jed was swiftly explaining the situation and telling his plan. The crew would spread out and make a loose cordon around the outbuildings. There were enough of them to form a complete circle with intervals of about fifty feet between each man. The lightning should provide enough visibility to ensure that the assassin wouldn't slip out between them.

"Hah," grunted Leandro Mirabel. "And then we jos' wait till he come out?"

"No," said Jed. "Six of us will move in and search the buildings. You, Leandro—Aaron, Rubio, Poke, Sam, and me."

"Ho, boy. That is good. But do we shoot to kill?"

Jed hesitated. "If you have to. But try to take him alive. We want to learn the why of this."

"Hah. Good."

Lightning lit up the rock-hewn features of Aaron Troop, hulking at Jed's elbow. Never before had Jed raised a voice of authority with the crew. Just now he'd done so without thinking. And full expected the big, assertive range boss to say something. But Troop was silent with his thoughts, his gaze slanted down.

"Come on then," Jed said curtly. He

headed for the outbuildings, adding a few more orders that fanned men out to his right and left to circle the structures. With his five men, Troop and Leandro and the others at his back, he moved down the mired lane that straggled between the buildings. Stables. Barns. Open-sided hay sheds. Each one had to be searched. You opened a door, then moved aside so as not to outline yourself, and waited for a lightning flare to wash the interior.

You saw nothing; you gave the order to move on.

The men's boots quickly balled with mud; they had to slog along slowly, half-floundering. Fans of rain slashed against their faces; lightning made white mirrors of the puddled ruts. Damn such conditions! The assassin had a gun, the confusion of rain and sky-lit murk might still help him to escape . . .

A rusty shriek pulled Jed up. The door of the slope-roofed tack shed hung open in the rainy wind, grating on its hinges. Left accidentally ajar? Or secured in clumsy haste and rocking open now?

Jed's spine tingled. He hesitated a moment, then called firmly: "You in there. Come on out!"

No reply. Jed pictured the inside of the old shed. It was full of crates and gear, and offered a number of hiding places. He wouldn't determine anything just by peering inside; he'd have to make a corner-by-corner search.

"Ho, maybe he ain' there," Leandro muttered. "But we go look, hah?"

"The hell with that," Troop said. "Shoot into the walls, he'll come out or—"

"No," Jed said flatly. "I want him alive . . . if that's possible. I won't ask anyone to risk his life. All of you stand back. I'm going in."

"Hah. I come too," said Leandro.

"No. Stay here. But give me your gun."

Wordlessly Leandro handed him his pistol. Jed held it under his wet coat, out of the rain, as he tramped over to the shed. Pausing by the doorway, he squinted into the blackness. A runnel of water trickled coldly down his neck.

"One last chance. Come on out."

Straining his eyes, he made out dim stacks of boxes and gleams of tools lining the walls. Then he stepped swiftly into the warm gloom.

His nerves prickled to a soft noise.

Something bright-streaking rushed by his

head: a flung tool of some sort. It whirled out the door behind him.

Jed instinctively sidestepped. Tripped over a crate and crashed on his side in a tangle of boxes. Hearing a movement feet away, he tried to bring the pistol out of his coat, but the twisted cloth snarled his arm.

A thickset form lunged; steel flashed.

Jed rolled frantically away. Felt a blade slice through his clothing and glide like cold flame along his ribs. Then his attacker was leaping away, overturning a box as he dived out into the rain.

Jed scrambled to his feet and plunged out the door just as Troop bawled an order. The man was veering off from Jed's companions, lunging away between the buildings. Troop, Rubio and Sam all fired at once. The runner had covered perhaps thirty feet when the bullets slammed into his body. He plunged forward in his run, his body furrowing through the brown ooze till it came to a loose, sprawling stop with its face in a puddle.

Jed stumbled over to it. He started to lean down, then grimaced and straightened, pressing a hand to his left side. The searing ache told him that the knife had cut into the muscles above his ribs.

The men came up and stood staring down. Rain penciled their faces with bright streaks.

"Damn you, Aaron," Jed said thinly. "The others would have taken him—"

Troop bent and caught the dead man by an arm and flopped him over. Water glanced off his muddy face and ran into his open mouth. It was Bull Jack.

"There's your answer," Troop said. "We don't need to puzzle out his reasons."

"Ho, boy," Leandro sighed. "She's a tough old som bitch world. He is a fonny one, Bull Jock, but this I am not think of him."

Easing down on his haunches by the body, Leandro patted Bull Jack's pockets and then felt inside one. He gave a soft explosive grunt as he pulled out a tight roll of banknotes that was tied with a string. He held it out to Jed.

"Hah. Maybe this is what give him the real reason, no?"

Jed broke the string and fingered the bills out flat. "Five hundred in greenbacks." He lifted his gaze to the others. "He was put off this place a good while back. Did he hire on somewhere else?"

"Naw," grunted Sam. "Sincet your brother fired him, he been hanging around

Moratown. Was swamping out saloons and stables and the like for grub and guzzling money. He never saved up no wad like that, you can bet."

"This is so," Rubio nodded. "Even when he work here, always he blow his pay on whiskey."

Rain flattened the notes against Jed's palm. He gazed at them tight-lipped, his thoughts chilling with the full implications of this.

"It was for a pay-off," Perry said. "It was for a pay-off then."

He was slouched powerfully in an armchair, coat off and his right shirtsleeve rolled up. One of the bullets fired through the window had grooved a bloody furrow along his forearm. The women had put a bandage around it. Ceferina had hung a blanket over the broken window. Now she was sweeping up glass shards, clanking them into a pan, obviously eager to finish up and leave the room. Elizabeth was sitting on the edge of the settee, her face pale but composed.

"Perr, we don't know anything for sure," Jed objected.

Perry waggled his head. He'd been drinking continuously since the incident, which had shaken him somewhat. His hand was fisted around a full tumbler of whiskey; his voice was thick and bearish. "Jesus," he said, "what do you need? That busted-down bastard Bull Jack never saved a dollar after payday in his life. Five hundred dollars! He got paid in a lump to do a job on me. Sure he was riding a grudge, but it took the money to push a trilling bastard like him that far."

"There's still a question of who paid him."

"Like hell there is! Augustin Parral had the reason, all a man needs. And money. He has money. So he hired it done. Hired the one skunk in the country who wanted to nail my hide any way he could. Or Bull Jack went to Parral and offered his services—"

"You're pretty sure of that, eh?" Jed said dryly.

"What the hell you mean am I sure?"

Jed shrugged. "We haven't seen too much of you lately. The company you keep is your business. But you might have made an enemy or two you don't half suspect."

"Bull!" Perry said savagely. Swallowing the whiskey in three gulps, he rose, stalked to the sideboard and poured another. "It was Parral, nobody else."

"All right, Perr. If it makes sense to you

he'd risk bringing on a war by hiring you killed."

"Goddammit, use your head!" He tipped up the glass and drained it, then glared at Jed. "If Bull Jack had gotten me, there'd be no war. Get me without paying the price of open war—that was the whole goddam idea!" He swung around, pointing at Elizabeth. "You think that chicken-hearted witch'd do anything if I got killed? She wouldn't, any more than she'll do a goddamn thing about what happened just now. And Parral knows it."

Ceferina, looking frightened, hurried out of the room with the pan of broken glass Elizabeth sat very still, her eyes fixed on the wall. But only for a moment. Then she stood up with a hiss of skirts and walked to the portieres.

"Where hell you going?" Perry asked thickly.

She turned her face toward him. "I will not sit there and be a target for your abusive, filthy language. I am going to my room. To my old room. Where I intend to sleep from now on. Alone. Also I intend to keep the door locked."

"Go ahead," he jeered, rocking on his heels. "You're no damn use outside a bed anyway. Hell, you can't even get a kid started. Damn near five months and . . ."

Color rose in her face. "It could be you, Perry," she said clearly. "Did that ever occur to you?"

"Like hell it's me! You barren goddam witch, don't go trying to blame—!"

But he was shouting at an empty doorway. She had gone. Perry lifted the bottle from the sideboard, shambled back to his chair and collapsed into it. Hunched there like a blond bear, he stared at the floor and muttered to himself, taking a pull from the bottle now and then.

"Pen," Jed said, "you didn't mean to talk to Beth that way. You're drunk now and you'll be sorry later."

"I meant it. Goddammit, I meant it!"

I was only talking to myself, Jed thought with a sharpening sense of despair. God— how Perry had changed. Turning from careless to callous, then to openly brutal. It had all happened so quickly. Or had it? Had it been growing in him longer than Jed had ever wanted to see or admit?

Perry tilted the bottle and cursed. It was empty. He dropped it to the floor and got unsteadily to his feet. Stood swaying uncertainly, running a hand through his

rumpled mane, muttering, "Ah-h-h-h—"
Turning, he stumbled out through the portieres.

Jed sat where he was, listening to whisks of rain slap the roof. His thoughts were a bitter-black distillation of all that had happened, and suddenly he felt on the edge of decision. Tomorrow, he thought glumly. I'll leave tomorrow. For the moment he couldn't think beyond that. Didn't want to. Once he left here, he would have cut himself off from Perry, his last living tie, irrevocably and for good. Maybe this was what all his hesitation really boiled down to. But now his decision was fixed and he felt hollow-bellied with it. *Tomorrow* . . .

Faintly now, he heard Perry's voice from the bedroom corridor. Heard him say Elizabeth's name. Jed got up and tramped through the dining room, halting at the corridor entrance. Perry was standing in the hall in front of Elizabeth's old room, his hand on the doorlatch, rattling it.

"Beth," he mumbled. "You open up, hear? I'm your husband and I . . . I want to see you."

There was no answer. Perry stepped back, his shoulders hunched, staring at the door. "Goddammit," he roared, "you don't lock any doors against your husband! That's one thing you don't ever do!"

He raised a booted foot and drove it savagely against the door. Wood ripped and splintered; the door swung inward with a crash. Perry bulled forward into the room. Elizabeth gave a piercing scream. Jed was already in motion down the corridor, pivoting into the room. Perry had reached the bed; he swept out a hand to tear the blankets away.

Jed caught him by the shoulder and yanked him half around, then drove a fist into his face. It was a powerful full-armed blow that sent a jolt of pain clear to his shoulder. Perry slammed into the wall, his head rapping against it. Then went glassy-eyed as he sagged slowly down the wall and toppled on his side. Blood puddled from his broken lips on the floor. The skin of Jed's hand was split; he gingerly worked the knuckles and found that none were dislocated.

He looked at Elizabeth in the lamplight. She was sitting up in bed, the terror in her eyes fading to a gray bitterness now. With one hand she pushed the loose mass of her hair away from her face, holding the open throat of her nightgown shut with the other.

"That was the end," she whispered. "There's nothing left now."

"He was drunk," Jed said.

"Oh God, don't. It's deeper than that and you know it. Don't defend him any more."

Jed shook his head. "I'm not. I meant to tell you in the morning. I'm leaving here, Beth."

"That's very wise," she said bitterly. "How I wish that I could I do the same. But I made the bargain, bad as it was."

"*You* leave? It's still your ranch."

"I wish to God it weren't. Father was right. He said I'd stayed here because of him . . . and then there was Perry. Now there's nothing."

"Then sell the place. Clear out. Go wherever you want."

"No." Her face smoothly tightened. "I don't run that easily. Any more than Father ever did." Her eyes turned on Perry. "I don't feel any differently about him, Jed. That's strange, isn't it? But I won't take any more such treatment as this from him. Will you help me get him to bed? Then I'll want to speak with Aaron Troop."

Chapter 15

"I reckon this makes it pretty sure," Aaron Troop said. "That first bunch they killed off wasn't just a tickle in the ribs. Neither was them shots Bull Jack taken at Starbuck. This here makes it pretty sure. They mean real business."

"You mean Parral, hah?" said Leandro Mirabel.

"Who else?"

Troop, Leandro, and Poke Tanner were deep in the chaparral on TH's southeast range. They sat their horses and gazed down at the carcass of a slaughtered longhorn. Nor was it the only one. They had discovered five more dead cows scattered through the tangle of mesquite and greasewood.

Troop had had the crew riding tally on this end of the range; it was Poke who had discovered the first bullet-killed cow and had reported it to the range boss. Thereupon Troop had begun his own search of the back brush, taking Leandro and Poke along. They had quickly found other dead animals, wantonly shot to death like the ones Leandro and Jed Starbuck had come on a couple weeks back . . .

"Yeh," Poke said. "Seems pret' clear, don't it? We are hard by the Parral top range and that don't hardly seem no accident."

"Jee-zos," Leandro murmured. "This is the foolish thing, I think. *Stupido.* What are they trying to do?"

"See how far we can he pushed, I reckon," Troop said grimly. "First that other bunch, now this one. That try at Starbuck too. Don't figure there's much doubt. All them thing got paid for. It was Parral money that got paid."

"But we got to be sure, Aaron," Leandro argued. He pointed at the ground. "See, there is plent' track. She say is jos' one man who do this. The other time it was the same. Jed Starbuck and me follow one man, bot we lose track. Maybe this, we can follow her where she go, hah?"

Troop nodded curtly. "We'll do that . . . just to be sure. But I don't figure there's much doubt where it goes."

"Yeh, you got to face it, Leandro," grinned Poke. "Some Mex done it. That's all they got on that Parral place."

"*Hijo de puta!* Shut you big mouth."

Leandro's rejoinder held no rancor. The

badinage between friends so good as he and Poke was often rough and insulting and meant nothing. Yet he glowered a little. Poke was right: he did not like to think that *vaqueros* had done such a thing. It was a great shame and a waste of good meat.

The three men followed the tracks through the chaparral. The single horseman's sign twisted and turned in the heavy growth and it was slow going. Leandro, best tracker in the trio, frequently dismounted to study the trail. He could not yet make an intelligent guess about the rider's destination. Apparently this *chingado* had ridden quite aimlessly through the dense cover on the look-out for any strays that crossed his path. He hadn't been selective as to sex or age—he had simply shot any animals he'd come across. And apparently for no other reason than Troop had surmised: to goad TH like a fly lodged in a bull's ear. If it didn't make too much sense, well, maybe the *bastardo* who had ordered it was a little mad. It was easy to see how this might be. To strip a man of his *macho* as Starbuck had done to Augustin Parral was a thing that would surely fry his guts with hatred . . .

As the brush began to thin away somewhat, the tracks seemed to meander generally southward. Leandro was soon sure of it. Beyond a doubt, the rider was heading onto Parral land. Yet Leandro dismounted still again and sat on his haunches for a long while, pondering the clear prints. Something about them bothered him mightily.

"Well?" Troop said edgily. "You got a bug up your butt or some'at? What's the sign say?"

"She say this man he is go to Parral range." Leandro frowned. "Hah. Bot som'thing here, she is goddom fonny."

"What's 'at?" Poke asked.

"I don' know. I can't put my finger on her. *Por Dios.* Ain' that a som bitch, though."

"Come on," Troop said impatiently. "Let's follow it a ways farther. Far enough so's there's no mistake."

The brush fell behind them except for thin scatterings. Now the humpy scape dwindled down toward a short flat valley called Quintero Basin. It was a *playa,* one of the shallow lakes that dried up in the summer. The heavy rains of a couple weeks back had somewhat restored this one, but the vegetation around its rim remained a withered brown.

Leandro sleeved sweat from his face.

"Quintero. She mark the boundary with Parral, no?"

"That's right," Troop said. "But we'll go a little farther yet. If that jasper's track heads straight into Parral land, it's a dead sure thing."

Leandro nodded reluctantly. Something about this business, the feel of it in his bones, was not right. But he could not fault Aaron's reasoning. They must be sure.

The horseman's prints showed he had dipped into the valley. Here, for the first time, Leandro ran into trouble. The heavily mineraled soil of the basin floor had often been soaked by rising water which had receded to let the sun pound and shrink the naked earth till it was rock-hard and seamed with cracks. And impervious to prints.

"Looks like he was headed straight across," Poke observed. "We should pick him up again t'other side."

"Maybe," said Troop. "Other hand, he might of deliberately hit this stretch to cover his trail, then angled out of here in most any direction. All right. Means we will have to skirt around the whole basin to find where he come out. Save time if we split apart. I'll work around the north side, you two around

233

the south. We'll meet on the other side from here."

Leandro said: "What if we find the track?"

"Fire one shot. Then stay where you are till I get over there. I'll do the same."

They broke apart, Troop swinging along the right rim of Quintero Basin, Leandro and Poke along the left. Within a minute the two parties were hidden from sight of each other by the high yet gentle ridges that cradled the *playa* on all sides. The ridges were thinly overgrown with scrub oak and brazil brush, the soil underfoot loose but stony. Leandro and Poke rode slowly between the brush clumps, Leandro bending deep from his saddle to scan the ground for prints. They would not show easily on this gravelly earth, and he must be watchful. *Por Dios* . . . he wished he could think of what it was that didn't seem right about those hoofprints.

Poke dug out some makings, built a quirly and wiped a match alight on his shiny-worn chaps. "Lemme know if you find anything."

Leandro glanced at him, grumbling back mockery: "Hah, what a lazy *bastardo*. All you Anglos are lazy no-good *bastardos*. Just want sit in sun all day and say, ah, *mañana,* she is good enough for me."

Poke flipped the smoking match away, grinning around his cigarette.

Leandro grinned too, then returned his gaze to the ground. Poke was a good man, he thought with affection. It wasn't often that a man could feel on such easy terms with a gringo. Leandro had had the same good feeling with Jed Starbuck after a time. At first he'd felt toward the younger man as a father or a teacher might; this was a green boy who had needed teaching. Then, seeing a man break out of the boy's soft mold, Leandro had come to respect him, even as his respect for the older Starbuck had faded.

Hijo de puta! Life was strange. Leandro thought of that night two weeks back, when Bull Jack had been killed trying to kill Perry Starbuck. How afterward, as the crew had been settling down for sleep, Jed had awakened them. Miss Elizabeth had wanted to see Aaron Troop at once, and Troop had promptly gone to the house. Later the crew had learned that she'd told Troop she wanted a guard in the house at all times, as she was no longer safe with her husband. Since then, there was always a man on watch in the place.

The morning after this great fuss, Jed Starbuck had departed TH after bidding

Leandro and his other friends on the crew farewell. Leandro had been sorry to see him go, even though Jed might be going, he had said, no farther than the ranch of Arturo Mariel. If Arturo could provide him with honest work, he would stay. Such had been the case, Leandro had since learned, and Jed was living with the Mariels. He was a good gringo.

But *ai-yi!* That brother of his. Leandro's view of Perry Starbuck had by now shifted to complete contempt. Since Miss Elizabeth had taken away his authority and was treating him like a stranger, Starbuck had gone from bad to worse. He came and went as he pleased, but he no longer had the power to speak for TH and everyone in the country knew it. This had turned him even more sour and ugly, and much of the time he was *borracho,* drunk out of his head. Yet—at first he had been a strong leader, and the crew had taken to him. It was a pity that a taste of power had turned him into a nasty bully.

Yes, Leandro mused, it was often strange how things in life turned out. Yet life had been good to give him friends like Poke Tanner, like Rubio Perez, like Jed Starbuck. Life . . .

". . . trouble with you Mexes," Poke was saying, "you all—"

A shot made a splitting report. It shook echoes from the ridges. But Poke did not hear it. He was already slumping out of his saddle, his face a blood-shattered mask.

Leandro was frozen for an instant. Then instinctively reined in his mount and grabbed at his friend as he started to fall. Saw with a shock of horror that the back of Poke's head was gone. Leandro let go and jerked back and watched Poke's body drop between their horses.

A sense of his own danger struck Leandro. He quickly wheeled his horse around, shouting as he clapped in spurs and slammed the animal into a run. The nearest cover was a gravelly dip whose bottom was covered with scrub oak. Leandro streaked across the few yards that separated him from it. He was on its edge when a bullet smashed into his chest at an angle.

In the tearing pain of it he was only dimly aware of falling sidelong. Of hitting the brink of the swale and then rolling down its flint-strewn incline till he crashed into the oak thicket.

Leandro lay face down in the twigs and leaves, his body gouged by the knotty oak stems that had stopped his fall. He dimly heard the pound of hoofs as his horse ran away. Pain ran through his chest like a hot poker. *Dios. . . Dios!* This was nothing a man would walk away from. But he was not dead yet.

His face was pressed against the hot pebbles. With a mighty effort he turned his head so that he could see up the incline. The clustering foliage covered his body and also cut off his view except for the broken passage where he had plunged through. He could see nothing but a small patch of gravelly slope and blue sky above. That was all. But the one who shot me will come this way. He will come, Leandro thought. He will have to make sure of me . . .

Mustering his strength, Leandro excruciatingly turned his body sideways till he faced the patch of daylight. Arrowlike pain stabbed him from chest to back; his shirtfront was soaked with blood. *Dios . . .* give me this strength.

Bracing his left elbow against the ground, he gritted his teeth and slowly inched his upper body high enough for his elbow to support his half-lifted weight. With his right hand he groped for the Smith & Wesson snugged against his right hip, easing it free of leather. He cocked it with a hooked thumb and cradled it against his chest, the barrel tilted up. Now. Now, you *bastardo.* Now you can come find me. I will see you first. Then I will see you in hell . . .

A warm haze of sunlight smoldered down through the leaves; flinty points of light glanced off the naked slope. Leandro's eyes hurt; his chest keened with fire and he felt weary clear to his bones. His mind swam in amber warmth that threatened to funnel away his last awareness. He fought it with an iron concentration, putting all his attention on the slope.

There . . . the killer would show himself there. He would come down to look.

With an odd sudden clarity, a total picture flickered into Leandro's brain. Those hoofprints. What had been wrong about them. *Dios* . . . of course. He began to smile. The prints had showed one shoe built up with a couple of caulks on the inside. He knew the horse that had those tracks. It belonged to the TH string.

"Ain' that a som bitch, though," Leandro whispered.

For now he knew. Not the why, but who.

Boots crunched softly along the rise of land above. Leandro braced. He heard the killer pause back from the slope rim. To look at Poke's body, he thought. Come on, *bastardo*. Come on.

Again the crunch of steps. The boots came into sight at the top of the bank. Above the boots, his roof leaves cut off Leandro's view. But the killer could not see any of him, he knew. Only a trail of disturbed gravel where he had rolled downward. He will have to see more. Come closer, *amigo*. Ah. That is it . . .

The boots were starting down the incline. Chap legs came into sight, a rifle swinging in a hamlike fist, a heavy torso. Leandro's pistol moved till his sights crossed the broad chest. Aaron Troop's agate-cold eyes shone in the hat shadow cutting a tan slant across his upper face. Then he hung hard against the incline, heels dug in to halt his descent.

His stare found Leandro. A grunt of surprise left him. He started to bring up his rifle.

Leandro pulled the trigger.

The jolt of the bullet flung Troop around like a sawdust doll. He pitched face down against the sloping gravel. It rolled slickly under his weight so that he slid downward several feet, then lay motionless.

"Welcome to hell, *amigo*," Leandro whispered.

His straining arm relaxed. The pistol clinked on the gravel. His body sagged and sank. He knew a great wash of red darkness. And that was all he knew.

Troop lay half-conscious against the gravel slope. He didn't know for how long. His whole body seemed numb with the shock of the bullet. Slowly the numbness receded; he moved his arms and legs. Pain sawed through his guts below his right ribs. *Christ Jesus!* He waited for the first violent throb to subside, wondering if he'd be able to stand.

He had to. Couldn't leave the thing half finished. Must get back to TH. And somehow keep his swimming wits about him so that he could carry the rest of it through successfully. *Goddammit!* The whole thing could have gone so easily, so neatly. In fact it had, up till now. Well, he had nobody but himself to blame. Should have been more careful . . .

Troop slowly turned his head till he could see down into the thicket below his feet. Leandro lay still, his face against the ground. Should have got him dead on the shot,

241

Troop thought. The way he'd gotten Poke. But a moving target was something else, and a clean instant kill was always in doubt. Well, Leandro was done now. And so would he be unless he could force himself to get up and move.

Slipping one hand under his belly, Troop clamped it tight over the sand-caked wetness of his shirt. He pressed the other hand palm-flat on the gravel and slowly pushed himself up till he could get a knee under him. Doubled nearly over, he staggered to his feet and climbed the bank, driving his boots hard against the loose soil.

Reaching the top, he fell to his hands and knees. He stared vaguely at Poke's body lying a few yards away. Wondered if he had enough left to reach his horse. He looked muddily around him in hopes of spotting either Leandro's mount or Poke's nearby. Then he remembered that both animals had bolted away. He'd just have to try to reach his horse.

Again he got to his feet, feeling as if weights were attached to every part of his body, tugging him groundward. He stumbled along the flinty rises that edged the *playa*, holding his gut and trying not to fall. A savage chuckle rippled through his chest, savaging his belly with pain that made him grimace. But he kept chuckling. He had all of them fooled. All these goddam fools. This wound, in fact, would be a helluva convincer if it didn't kill him first. Nothing could be better for helping bear out his story . . .

Troop saw his horse standing where he'd left him, ground tied by a greasewood. Down one slope, up another, and he would be there. But staggering downward, he fell and went sprawling to the bottom. He lay on his stomach, hands clamped under him, fighting back waves of pain. His thoughts went soupy and sluggish, the hot nerve bends of purpose threading away. Can't get up . . . not yet . . . rest.

No.

Thought of Starbuck had crossed his mind. That was all he needed. Just to think of Perry Starbuck. Hatred twanged in his brain like a taut wire. It was enough to drive him back to his feet, tramping on and upward now. If, by God, this hole in the guts was going to kill him, let it wait. *First there was Starbuck.*

He reached his horse, lurching heavily into the animal and grabbing at the saddle leather. Troop leaned against it for a half-minute, holding to the saddle with a grip like death. Then, summoning all his bull-like stamina, he toed into stirrup and swung his leg up and over, settling his weight into the hull.

He heeled the horse into motion. And drifted with it like a man clinging to a raft in a gray and endless sea . . .

"There's no mistake, eh?" Starbuck demanded. "You're damned sure."

Troop's head stirred weakly against the pillow. "Yeah. Sure as sunrise. We was right on the line between TH and Parral land. Or a little over it. Not by much, but seems that was enough."

"All right." Starbuck glanced at Elizabeth, who was standing in the doorway. "Tell it again. I want her to hear it."

"Perry, I heard him the first time." Her mouth was pinched and pale. "What happened is more than clear enough."

Starbuck's eyes squinted to slits. "What happened is what I warned you all along would happen. You didn't listen. Now you can hear it again. Every word of it. Go on, Troop, tell it."

"Like I said," Troop whispered. "These *vaqueros* came riding up on us from the south. Four of 'em. We tried to talk, but they wasn't having any. They opened fire. Killed Poke and Leandro straightway. I took a bullet in my brisket, but held on and got out o' there. Lucky I had some o' the boys working that part of our range and I ran into a couple of 'em. They brung me in. Some o' the others are fetching in Poke and Leandro."

"That was *their* warning to *us,* I take it," Elizabeth said bitterly.

Starbuck whirled on her, half-lifting a clenched hand. "Goddammit, don't try to throw what's happened on me! Last thing I did was to deadfall that Parral bunch when they'd have raided our pens. They've made two strikes against us since, killing cattle on our land. And don't ever tell me it wasn't Augustin Parral that hired Bull Jack to get me. We let Parral get away with all that. You let him. So then he knew he could do anything he pleased. So now Mirabel and Tanner are dead."

"Go easy there," Troop husked.

Starbuck's flat gaze shuttled to him. "All right, what do you say? You took a bullet proving how right she was."

"Don't," Elizabeth whispered. "Don't, Perry! Stop it."

"Don't you want to hear if Troop's ready

to turn the other cheek? Go on, Troop, say it."

Troop let his eyes droop wearily shut. "I reckon there's times you have got to stand fast. Fight if need be. Ain't a matter of liking to. Man don't stand up for what's his, there is always someone going to take it away from him."

"I'm going to put it to the crew just like that," Starbuck said. And started toward the doorway.

"I forbid it," Elizabeth said in a chill voice.

Starbuck halted and looked at her. "You do that. You forbid the hell out of it. By now they all know how two of their bunkies were killed. How their range boss got shot in the belly. They've had a chance to put it all together. We'll see who they listen to now."

He walked out of the room.

Elizabeth stood biting her lip for a moment, and then she hurried after him. "Perry! *Perry*—"

Troop gazed at the ceiling, listening to her angry remonstrations as the two of them passed through the house and outside. A smile twitched his lips. He pressed a hand over the bandages covering his right side, then let go of a quiet chuckle. Its spasmodic pull on muscles in his torn-up gut hurt like hell. But he didn't mind. He didn't mind at all.

Chapter 16

"Why you left doesn't matter," said Elena. "What is important is that you did leave."

"I don't know," Jed said. "Can it be that simple?"

"It always is. People give themselves all sorts of reasons for feeling this way or that. The reasons don't matter. They may be true. Or false. All that counts is what one does. His actions are what bear him out."

The two of them were standing by Arturo Mariel's horse corral, watching a pair of colts frisking around the compound. The puffs of dust they stirred up made a pinkish haze in the last sunrays. Tonight the sun was bleeding itself slowly into extinction, casting a red glow over the land. It curved along Elena's profiled cheek as she smiled a little, watching the colts' antics. She'd thrown a *rebozo* around her shoulders against the twilight's early chill. Now she turned her head to meet Jed's eyes, and her face was serious.

"In some ways your brother is like my brother," she said. "Both are strong in all the wrong ways; both are ruthless. But Perry Starbuck is rash where Augustin is cautious. He takes chances that Augustin never would. That headstrong way is dangerous, I think, in a ruthless man."

"Dangerous to himself," Jed muttured.

"Yes. And to those around him. You did well to get away from him. Why doesn't matter."

Still, Jed had thought about it a lot. Part of the reason he'd left Perry was that he could no longer dredge up excuses for him. More important, he thought, he'd always been cowed by Perry in a way. He'd been the younger brother too long. Since they had come to Texas, he had been realizing his own way as a man more and more.

At Arturo Mariel's, he'd learned new values in which to anchor his life. Arturo's wasn't a large house, but it was large in hospitality, in trust, in friendship. When he had come here from TH, the Mariels had taken him in on trust; it was enough that Elena had greeted him as a friend.

As if she'd read his thoughts, Elena broke

the silence gently: "You have worked hard these weeks, Jed. You've more than paid your way."

"I don't think so. But I've tried. There are some things . . ." He shrugged, a little embarrassed. "Things you can't simply pay off for."

She nodded, smiling. "I've felt the same. We're a pair of mavericks, but we've found a place. The same place. Strange, isn't it?"

She was saying what had been on his own mind of late. That at the Mariels' he had found a sense of rooted contentment such as he'd never known. The life was hard, the working hours long, but he couldn't begin to measure what more this family's simple earth-loving ways had given him.

For Elena, it was the same. Soon she'd have faced a day that any marriageable girl of her station must: stiffly facing a rows of stiff-faced young suitors, a stiff-backed *duenna* in attendance. A day she'd dreaded the thought of. With it would go the few freedoms she'd enjoyed. Particularly the long rides she'd loved to take alone because they'd blunted, somehow, a nameless ache she had never been able to define. Until the day of her liberation: coming to live with the Mariels. Not that it followed that everyone would find what she had in this hard essential way of living, she'd told Jed seriously. It was right for her, an affirmation of her life, her being. That was all she was sure of.

Thinking of this, and of Elena herself, Jed had come to a conclusion. Several conclusions, really. He'd done a lot of careful thinking about them. And he judged that the time had come to speak up.

"I've got some money coming from Perry," he said.

"Have you?"

"I invested it in TH. He said he'd return it whenever I asked for it."

"Oh? But will he?"

"Sure. Perry keeps his word, give him credit for that. I've been thinking . . ." Jed leaned straight-armed on a corral pole, gripping it so hard his hands ached. He didn't look at her. "Be nice to have a place like Arturo's. Land and cattle, but not too much. You wouldn't want a big place, would you?"

"Whose wants are we discussing?"

"All right—" He dropped his hands, walked to her and caught her by the shoulders, turning her to face him. "I am talking about you too. Could you see your way to sharing it with me . . . as my wife?"

"Why, Jed?"

"Why, well, we're both alone, we've no place of our own, I think we could have a good life together. Anyway, I . . . I love you, 'Lena."

"I love you too. That's what needed saying. What we both needed to hear. The other things . . ." She smiled slowly. "I think we can take those for granted, Jed."

They stood together for a long time. Jed wasn't conscious of the passing of time until, half-startled, he became aware that a horseman was coming this way. The red light had melted to a beige dusk, and he couldn't make out anything but a hard thrumming of hoofs which indicated that the rider was already close.

Jed felt a stab of premonition. Nobody would run a horse that way without a reason. Not at this hour. The door of the Mariels' adobe house opened; candlelight spilled into the yard. Arturo Mariel's stocky form filled the doorway, light streaking the barrel of his rifle. From inside, the children made sleepy, querulous sounds.

"What is it?" asked Arturo.

"One rider," said Jed. "Can't pick him out yet."

Lupe's voice was raised sharply: "Husband, don't stand in the light."

Arturo conceded the wisdom of this advice by stepping out into the yard and pulling the door shut behind him. He moved over by Jed and Elena as the rider came around the corral at a lope. "Whoa!" It was Elizabeth Starbuck's voice; she careened her hard-ridden mount to a halt.

Jed stepped up to her stirrup. "It's me, Beth. Jed. What's happened?"

"Jed . . . Jed!"

She bent from her saddle and he swung her to the ground. Dusty and disheveled, exhausted and trembling, she leaned against him, clutching his arms. "I couldn't stop them," she said in a broken whisper. "God, oh God, I tried to reason with them."

"Stop who? From what?" Jed seized her elbows, giving her a hard shake. "Make sense!"

He pieced the story together from her disconnected speech. Aaron Troop brought in badly wounded. Telling how he, Poke, and Leandro had been attacked close to the Parral line, both Leandro and Poke killed. Troop verifying that the attackers had been Parral *vaqueros!* The news had clinched one fact for Perry: that Augustin Parral had declared open war. Giving TH all the excuse needed to take direct full-scale action. Overriding Elizabeth's objections, he'd taken his argument to the crew. Already fired up by the shootings of Leandro and Poke, they'd required little persuasion. And they had ridden out in a body, Perry at their head . . .

"I tried to talk them out of it," Elizabeth said wildly. "They wouldn't listen. Not a single man would listen to me! God, I tried everything, even told them all of them were through at TH. Jed!" She caught blindly at him again. "You've got to stop him!"

Jed stood as he was, feeling cold-sick in his guts. Leandro his friend. With an effort, he pulled his glance to her, saying tonelessly: "What makes you think he'll listen to me?"

"Please. You've got to try!"

"I can understand how the men feel," Jed muttered.

"Yes! And how do you like your brother becoming a murderer?" Elizabeth almost screamed the words at him. "There'll be shooting! There's bound to be! Do you want more blood on his hands?"

Arturo Mariel, unable to follow the impassioned English, queried Elena. She replied in Spanish. "Ah," sighed Arturo, and shook his head. "Then there's nothing to be done. If the gringo and his men left before the señora did, they're already halfway to the Parral *hacienda*. Too late, even, for Jed to stop the TH men, if this could be done."

"But we can't just do nothing!" Elizabeth sobbed.

Elena laid a hand on Jed's arm. "It's not nearly as far from here to the *hacienda* as it is from TH to there. If you ride very fast, there may be a chance."

"Not on that slope-hipped cayuse of mine."

"You can take my Star. He's made for speed and will run his heart out."

"How will Jed find his way by night to a place he's never been?" Arturo objected.

"You have one very fast horse of your own, Cousin," said Elena. "Will you guide him?"

"Yes, gladly."

He couldn't do less than try, Jed decided. While Arturo hurried to prepare the horses, he went to the small 'dobe bunkhouse he shared with Arturo's two *vaqueros*. He told them that Arturo needed their help with the horses; both men exited. Jed dug through his plunder till he located his 1860 Colt Army pistol. Biting the ends off six paper cartridges, he loaded the chambers. He rammed the .44-caliber balls home with the loading lever and fitted percussion caps to the nipples. Shoving the weapon into his belt now, he quickly returned to the corral. Arturo and his men were saddling the two mettlesome horses, savagely cursing them. One by one, they snubbed the animals to the post and got the saddles on.

Elizabeth was crying quietly. Elena had an arm around her friend's shoulders.

Elena's lifting gaze met Jed's. She left Elizabeth and came over to him. "I should be going with you," she said.

"You stay here. And keep Beth here too." He paused, isolating the bleak conviction of his next words. "I've a feeling that one of our brothers will be dead before this is over. Or it will never be over. Unless I can stop it. Somehow . . ."

"Jed . . ." Elena's teeth caught her lower lip. "If talking doesn't help, don't be foolish. Don't risk—"

"I can't make any promises. Perry has to be stopped. I have to try—one way or the other."

"Oh, *por Dios!* Then be careful. Please—"

Jed moved to the corral gate and took the reins that a *vaquero* held out to him. Arturo was right behind him as he heeled Star into movement, heading south. Only a faint afterglow showed along the darkening rim of land.

The two of them set a driving pace through the night hours. They couldn't chance a breakneck run in this near dark, but Arturo knew the country as he did the seams of his palm. They made good time, which improved as the half moon's hazy glow intensified. Yet Jed thought that the miles crept by slowly.

He found himself aching with worry for the brother he'd never really understood. It seemed that a man could never wholly cut himself off from the blood tie. And now? Jed wasn't sure what he'd do if he and Perry had a confrontation that couldn't be resolved except by a head-on clash. How far are you willing to go? he wondered. And knew there'd be no answer till the moment came . . .

Arturo reined in, lifting his hand. "Listen."

The popping of gunfire was faint with distance, yet distinct in the clear night. Jed felt a constriction around his chest.

"Is that at the Parral place?" he asked.

"The shots come from that way. *Andale!*"

Arturo dug in his spurs, racing his horse down a wide *barranca.* Jed was right behind him. The two emerged from this clear runway onto a brushy ridge. The horizon ahead seemed to bloom with a fanning reddish glow.

Jed glanced at his companion. "Fire?"

Arturo's wry brown face puckered up like wrinkled leather. "You are too late. If there was anything you could have done.

"There may still be."

Jed gigged his horse down the rise. Arturo reined on past him, and once more took the lead. The shooting had stopped; it did not pick up again. Apparently, Jed thought hopefully, TH's attack on the *hacienda* had not resolved itself into a siege or long-drawn battle. The Parral people would have been abed and wholly unprepared; Perry must have had little difficulty taking them by surprise. But having swiftly seized control, he'd already ordered some buildings fired. No telling what he might do next.

It seemed a long time before Jed and Arturo topped a long bare hummock north of the Parral headquarters. The scene below them was brightly lighted by fire leaping from the roof of every building in sight. The adobe walls would not burn, but the pole-and-thatch roofs were sheeted in flames.

Jed murmured, "Come on," and they rode toward the buildings.

At the edge of firelight, a sharp voice hailed them. "*¡Alto!*" The voice belonged to Rubio Perez. He came tramping out of the shadows of some nearby trees, a rifle cradled on one arm. "*¿Quien es?*"

"Jed Starbuck," said Jed. "This is Arturo Mariel."

Rubio nodded curtly. "I know him. How do you hear of this?"

"From Miss Elizabeth."

Jed stepped to the ground, sweeping his gaze across the great yard. Roofs afire everywhere: barns, outsheds, a row of adobes that were *peones'* dwellings. Only the big house remained untouched. Men and women had dragged their meager belongings, furniture, bedding, utensils, out of the burning shacks. They stood in silent groups, watching their roofs go on smoke. Children wept fretfully; women comforted them with liquid murmurs. Another sound keened above the crackle of flames: the high uncontrollable wailing of a woman in grief. She was kneeling by a blanket-covered form.

Jed said: "Her husband?"

Rubio nodded, grim-jawed. "We took this place by surprise, but still there was shooting. Two of us were wounded, two of them. That *vaquero* was killed."

"Was he one of the four that got Leandro and Poke?"

"*Quién sabe?* We do not know who those four were." Rubio's voice was brittle with regret and anger. "These people deny that any of their men did such a thing. I do not know . . .

Jed remembered how close Rubio and Leandro had been. Across the yard, a line of weaponless half-dressed men, Parral *vaqueros,* stood sullen-faced under the guns of the TH crew. He wondered how many bellies of the latter were starting to sour with the bleak remorse that Rubio felt. They had acted in the fire of an angry impulse; now a man who was probably innocent was dead. Leaving a widow and no doubt children to mourn him. And they were just as innocent . . .

"Where is my brother?"

"He went into the house." Rubio shrugged. "What happens there . . . it is no affair of ours."

"I'm making it mine," Jed said quietly.

"I'm going in there, Rubio. Any objections?"

"I? None. I don't give a damn what any Starbuck does. Or any Parral either." His eyes glinted; he gestured toward the Parral *peones*. "These are my people. Do what you please, gringo. Go in the house if you will. If none of you leave it alive, some good will yet come from this night."

Jed headed for the house, pistol in hand. He was prepared for anything, but nobody challenged him. He crossed the patio and paused at the entrance of a gloomy corridor. Ahead of him, lamplight framed a doorway. Quiet voices reached him: Perry's and Augustin Parral's.

"There's a gun." Perry's voice was slurred and savage. "Pick it up!"

"Go to hell, Anglo." Augustin's tone was calm, judicious, mocking. "I do nothing that gives you satisfaction. Kill me as I am. For you it should not be hard."

"You'll pick that gun up, by God, or I'll shove it in your—"

Jed reached the door and stepped into the room; Perry half-wheeled toward him.

"Christ! What are you doing here?"

"It ought to be obvious," Jed said thinly.

"Beth ran and told, eh? Did she think you could stop me?"

A gun was holstered at Perry's hip. Jed felt an ooze of sweat between his palm and the pistol grip. God, he thought, did it have to be? A final showdown with Perry? He groped for words.

"Perr . . . what proof do you have he ordered Leandro and Poke killed?"

"Jesus, don't start on that again! He ordered it. Who else would?"

"What does he say?"

"He denies it, goddam it! What did you think?"

Jed edged a glance at the bed. Augustin was sitting up, light silvering the grotesque scars on his face. A gun shone on the rumpled coverlet by his feet. Perry must have tossed it there. Augustin's eyes were avid; he seemed to derive some warped and ironic satisfaction out of a situation in which Perry had absolute mastery. And Perry's face was twisted with a baffled fury.

"You've got one innocent man killed tonight," said Jed. "One's enough."

Perry showed his teeth. "There are no innocent in this rattler's nest. I'm going to clean it out. Starting with the king rattler."

"How will you do it, Perr? Same as with

him? Line up those women and babies out there and shove guns at 'em and tell 'em to defend themselves?"

"Don't crowd me any more, boy—"

Perry's voice had turned low and dangerous. He swung on his heel until he was fully facing Jed. In that instant, Augustin Parral moved like a striking snake. His extended arm shot toward the pistol on the coverlet.

Jed's eyes flicked past Perry's shoulder. *"Watch out!"*

The gun in his fist tipped up. He fired.

Augustin gave a strangled cry and fell back. Instant blood dyed the arm of his nightshirt. Perry had grabbed for his pistol as he saw Jed's gun come up. Now, hand still fisted around his undrawn weapon, he stared bewilderedly at Jed, then at Augustin, and at Jed again.

Walking straight up to Perry, Jed rammed his pistol muzzle against his belly. "That ends it, Perr. You hear me? You're not going to kill Parral. You pull that gun and I'll pull this trigger. I'll pull it, by God!"

Perry's head sank tight between his shoulders. A sheen of sweat grooved the creases between his jaws and neck. "All right," he said very softly. "This once. This one time, kid. But never stand in my way again. Never."

He took a step backward from the gun. Tramped around Jed and past him, and stalked out of the room.

Chapter 17

"Get Rufio." Augustin's voice was a scratchy hiss. "Get him in here, for the love of God!"

He was cradling his bloody arm against his chest, his scarred face even uglier in pain. Jed left the room and tramped out to the fire-lit patio. Perry, his voice taut with fury, was calling the TH men together. In a few moments, the war party had pulled back to its horses and was mounted and riding away. Tito Rozales was coming toward the patio at a swaying, tub-bellied trot. Seeing Jed standing beside the gateway, he halted.

"What's happened in there?" he demanded. "I heard a shot . . ."

"Parral's alive." A trembling reaction ran through Jed; he leaned a hand against the wall. "I shot him in the arm . . . if you want to make anything of that."

"You?" Tito's heavy brows drew together. "But . . . what of your brother?"

"He was going to kill Parral. I stopped it." Jed felt a weary lack of interest in the subject. "If you know anyone named Rufio, Parral wants him."

"The house servant." Rozales gave a contemptuous clack of his tongue. "An old fool frightened of his shadow. He will be hiding somewhere. I will see to the *patrón's* hurt myself."

He brushed past Jed and entered the house.

Rubio Perez and three other Mexicans of the TH crew had chosen to remain behind. They were helping the Parral people form a bucket brigade. Three confused lines assembled between the buildings and the nearby creek, but it was really wasted effort. By now the roofs were nearly consumed, the adobe beneath impervious to fire, and the people had removed the burnable objects from their dwellings.

Arturo Mariel had joined a bucket line, and Jed took a place beside him. The tired strain he felt wasn't at all physical; he was glad enough to plunge into this frenzied diversion. At such times people needed to occupy themselves at something, any sort of feverish activity, no matter how useless. He no less than anyone else . . .

For about an hour they helped labor to extinguish the different blazes. By then a predawn gray had started to tinge the east; a slow crawl of daylight was beginning. Jed and Arturo flung themselves down on the creekbank, sweaty, soot-smeared and exhausted. Arturo dipped up a double handful of water, rinsed his mouth and spat.

"Ahhh . . . I think we will go home now, eh?"

"I don't know," Jed muttered.

The violent reaction he'd felt earlier had drained away, leaving the dregs of a bitter dissatisfaction to cloud his thoughts. What had this confrontation with Perry really solved? Not a damned thing, he thought bleakly. He had merely thrown Perry off-stride this once. Sooner or later there'd be other acts of callous violence. And then . . . ?

Arturo nudged him. *"Mire* . . . look."

Four riders were moving up from the northwest toward the *hacienda.* From the direction of Arturo's place. Jed and Arturo rose and walked to meet them. The growing light picked out Elena and Elizabeth, and with them rode Arturo's two *vaqueros.* Elena pulled up her mount and looked about her.

At the charred remains that had roofed sheds and huts. At the destitute groups of *peones* gathered in the yard.

"Santa Maria . . . what has been done here?"

"Only what you see," Jed said. He briefly told what had happened and how he'd had to put a bullet in her brother's arm. "Nothing serious," he concluded.

"Thanks to Jed," said Arturo. "Perry Starbuck has come and gone; it is over. But you were told to stay home."

"We couldn't sit about waiting," Elena said tartly. "Besides you were gone too long."

Something bumped softly across the stones of the patio. It was Tito Rozales coming from the house, pushing Augustin Parral ahead in his wheelchair. The bandage on Augustin's arm made a pale blur in the dimness. At the gateway, he raised his crooked left arm to halt Tito. For a moment he stared unspeaking at their group.

"Good morning, fools," be said softly. "And goodbye."

"Your arm—" said Elena. "It's not badly hurt?"

"That, my dear Elena, is none of your business. Get out of here. Take your Anglo paramour and your other pig friends with you."

"You are the swine," Arturo Mariel said. "But for Jed Starbuck, you would be dead."

Augustin grinned grotesquely. "No fear, Cousin. That would be a mercy God won't permit." His eyes moved to Elizabeth. "Tell your husband that my money can hire *pistoleros* too. That I will be ready for his next visit."

"There will be no next visit," Elizabeth said quietly. "Perry Starbuck will never give another order at TH. I'll see to that. If you will keep the peace, so will we. I give my word."

"Ah—" Augustin's lip curled. "And I must accept a lady's word, eh? Very well, I accept it—and will be prepared when it's broken. Now get out, all of you."

"One thing," Jed said. "Nobody's holding a gun on you now. You know that somebody hired a man to shoot my brother. That two killing raids were made on TH cattle . . ."

"I ordered one raid on TH pens. The one my dear sister betrayed. Of the others, I know nothing. You fool! If I had given such orders, do you think your brother would have found us unprepared tonight? That we wouldn't expect retaliation?" Augustin's fin-

267

gers taloned around the arms of his wheel-chair; his voice dropped to a hiss. "Do you think I'd lie to your bastard of a brother to save my skin or for any reason? Get out!"

Jed and Arturo went to get their horses. With the women and the *vaqueros,* they rode away in the graying dawn. It was Elena who finally broke the silence.

"Augustin told the truth. I know him. It's not a thing he'd lie about."

"It's not really important," Elizabeth said wearily. "All the way here, 'Lena, I was thinking. I'm going to sell TH. Perhaps to your brother if he wants it. Or to anyone who can meet a reasonable price. And I won't wait to see it sold . . . I'll leave that matter to Perrin and Perrin, father's attorneys in Moratown."

"Where will you go, Beth?"

"To Virginia. Or Maryland. Mother had family in both places. I can make a new home among them. A new life."

"And Perry?" Jed asked.

"I don't care what he does. Let him do whatever he pleases. It doesn't matter any more."

Jed didn't believe it. He noted too that she'd made no mention of an annulment or divorce. But he didn't comment; it was no business of his. All he said was: "If you're going back to TH now, Beth, I'll ride with you."

"If you like. But why?"

"I've been thinking too. If you don't care any more, I still do. I care what happens to Perry. There's one way, just one I know of, to whittle him to size. Make him a little human again."

Elizabeth gave him a swift glance. Then tried to mask her spark of interest by feigning indifference. "Oh. Is there?"

Jed nodded. "By breaking his pride. And I know the way."

Elena reined close to him, her eyes shadowed by a quick worry. "Jed . . ."

"You go on to Arturo's. I'll be along soon." He reached out and caught her hand. "I have to do it, 'Lena. It's not what I want to do. Not to any man, least of all Perry. But it's got to be done."

The eastern gray had turned to a pearly sheen across the sky when Troop, half-dozing, heard incoming riders crossing the yard toward the corral. It took him a sluggish minute to drag himself fully awake. He turned his head, but the window beside his bed was too high for him to gaze out.

Setting his teeth, Troop inched himself up to a sitting position with small jerking movements, grunting with the dagger-like pain that shot through his gut at each jerk. But no mere pain, by God, could keep Aaron Troop on his back. Particularly since Leandro's bullet had gone clean through him without tearing up a vital organ. Even if some sharp effort reopened the wound, he wouldn't be hemorrhaging from any dangerous spot. The stiff girdle of bandages around his torso bothered him more than the hurt of his wound.

Maneuvering himself half upright, his back bolstered by pillows, Troop peered through the window. He saw two people coming from the corral. Elizabeth, sure, and it was no great surprise to see Jed Starbuck beside her. Troop had figured she might have gone to him last night after Starbuck and the men had departed for the Parral place. Only Troop and Cefedina had remained at TH headquarters. The housekeeper had told him where Starbuck and the crew had gone, but she'd no idea of the señora's destination.

Troop had also awakened a couple hours ago, when the crew had returned from their call on Augustin Parral. It had still been half dark then. He had heard voices out in the yard, these gradually dispersing as the crew retired to the bunkhouse. Perry Starbuck had come stamping into the house, savagely cursing and muttering. Something had gone wrong for him, Troop guessed, an opinion quickly confirmed by the repeated clinking of glass on glass from the *sala* as Starbuck poured and downed one drink after another. Troop had been bursting with curiosity, wondering if things had worked out according to his plan. But he'd firmly stifled curiosity, wanting to take no chances on arousing Starbuck's suspicions Or anyone else's. At last the sounds from the *sala* had ended as Starbuck had either gone to sleep or passed out. And Troop had dozed off again . . .

Now Troop watched narrow-eyed as Jed and Elizabeth walked toward the house. She must have gone to the Mariels' to enlist Jed's aid, but why had he come to TH with her? What had been going on all those intervening hours? Troop thrust his small suspicion aside as unworthy. He would ask Elizabeth what had happened; she'd have an honest, straightforward answer . . .

He heard Jed and Elizabeth enter the *sala*, their quiet voices, then Elizabeth's step coming down the hall. Softly she opened the door of Troop's room and then, seeing him awake and sitting up, came over to the bed.

"Aaron, you should be asleep . . . at least lying flat on your back. Here, let me arrange those pillows."

He was overwhelmingly conscious of her nearness as she leaned over him, strong brisk hands plumping the pillows at his back and then drawing the blankets up to his chest. She laid a cool palm on his forehead. "Very little fever. But you shouldn't be sitting up."

"I'm fine," he said tersely. "Woke up when you and young Starbuck rode in. What's going on?"

Before she could reply, Jed Starbuck's voice rose in sharp command out in the *sala:* "Get up, Perry!" A slapping sound. "Get up, I said!"

Troop scowled. "What the devil . . . ?"

Elizabeth smiled wanly. "Jed is about to fetch his big brother a lesson. Or so he says."

"How's that?"

"He plans to make a very large dent in Perry's pride. With a sound beating."

Troop jerked out a dour chuckle. "Kid's dreaming. He can't whip his brother."

She gave a small, weary shrug. "I don't

think he can either. But evidently he means to try."

Perry, roused from a drink-fogged sleep, was asking in a sleepy tumble what the hell was going on. Jed's answer was flat and uncompromising. There was a brief, incredulous silence. Then Perry laughed outright. "You've taken leave of your senses, kid. You really have!" But it seemed that Jed had learned a few choice words for making a challenge stick. Stock words, but he used them to biting effect. Both men's voices grew heated, as if some long-time tension had peaked between them. "All right, kid." Perry's tone was soft and unamused now. "If that's what it'll take to show you . . ."

Elizabeth had seated herself in the chair drawn up by Troop's bed. Her head was up as she tensely listened. Troop watched her fingers lace together till her hands were tightly knotted in her lap.

"What happened, Beth?" he asked quietly.

In a voice dull with indifference, she began to tell him of the night's events. Out in the *sala*, a door sharply opened and closed. Troop's glance moved to the window. Jed and Perry Starbuck walked into his view as they crossed the yard. Walking east toward a low rise that was darkly etched against the flush of true dawn. Taking their disagreement away from the house. But not very far away . . .

Elizabeth had finished speaking. Now, following the focus of Troop's attention, she skirted the bed and moved up by the window. Looking out, her face was oddly tranquil in repose. Even etched by tiredness and travail, it was a lovely face. As beautiful as the profile of her tall body in the morning light.

"Beth." His tongue felt thick and dry. "How much longer you going to put up with that damnyankee and his meanness?"

"No longer." She continued to stare out the window. "I'm sorry, Aaron . . . I forgot to mention it. But then I only decided a few hours ago. I am putting TH up for sale. Then I am leaving for the East."

It hit Troop like a small bombshell. For a moment he sat in stunned silence, digesting her words. Then he said hoarsely: "Leaving . . . for good?"

Elizabeth did look at him then; she said gently, "Yes, Aaron."

"What about Starbuck? You staying married to him?"

Her lips compressed, her eyes lowered. "I

don't know. What happens with Perry and me . . . depends on him now."

"He ain't going to change. He'll never be different than he is. You ought to know that by now."

"Please—Aaron. Let's not . . ."

"Let me say it. Just once let me say it." His voice cracked with a pleading intensity. "You know how I always felt about you, Beth, how I'd do anything for you, anything you ask. That has got to mean something. Tell me it means a little bit anyway, Beth, just tell me . . ."

"I can't."

She backed off slowly from the bed; her eyes seemed abnormally wide. Why, she was plain frightened. Frightened of what? Him? She shouldn't be frightened of him.

"Beth—"

"I can't, Aaron. It wouldn't be true. I'm sorry."

She turned quickly and went out the door, pulling it shut behind her.

For a long minute Troop stared blankly at the closed door. It had been for nothing, he thought. All for nothing. All for her, and none of it had meant a thing. The words repeated themselves over and over in his brain like a maniacal refrain.

Finally he scoured a hand roughly over his face.

. All right, then. All right.

He swung his weight toward the edge of the bed, teeth set against the pain. Then threw back the blankets and swung his feet to the floor. Holding a hand pressed to his belly, he got up slowly. Stood swaying for a wobbly moment. His lips stretched in an iron-faced grin. Yes, he could make it. He could still do what there was left to do.

Beth had gone out to the *sala*. He couldn't get out of the house that way. Didn't have to. The hallway ran straight back to an outside door. Be damned quiet about it, he could slip out that way unnoticed. His rifle? He tried to remember. Ah, he had left it at the spot where Leandro had shot him. But the crewmen who had brought in Leandro's and Poke's bodies would have brought it home. Where would they leave it? Where he always did. By his saddle in the harness shed . . .

His glance shuttled to his clothes hanging on a peg behind the door. Moving with infinite care, he made his way over to them.

"This all right with you?"

276

Perry's tone was sardonic; his mouth was tipped in a crooked grin. He wasn't taking any of this a damned bit seriously. Jed swung his gaze around the location. They were hundreds of yards from the headquarters, the long rise they had crossed cutting them entirely off from it. The sun thrusting up eastward slashed hazy pink beams across the short, curling grass.

Jed's glance went back to Perry; he nodded.

Both men shucked their coats, rolled them around their pistols and laid them aside in the wet grass. Squaring off then, they began to shift carefully around each other, fists slightly cocked, bodies stiff except for the movements of their feet. Both sidling a little toward the sun, each wary of being maneuvered so that the horizontal sunrays would hit his eyes. Perry still wore the side-tipped grin; his shoulders rolled powerfully under his vest and shirt.

He wasn't soft, but he had gone heavy; he was out of condition. For months he'd been eating too much and too well; he had been drinking heavily for weeks. During that time he had done little in the way of physical work; the months had smothered his hard bigness with tallowy weight. Meantime Jed had been getting his full growth, broadening out only where it counted, hardening out too. Facts that Perry either hadn't taken cognizance of or had contemptuously discounted. He still had an edge of sheer size and Jed didn't deceive himself that a few slack months had diminished his physical power very much. But all the extra weight Perry was packing should slow him some. Enough? That was the big question . . .

The pattern of their movements began to subtly change. Perry was shifting into a gradual offensive while Jed fell into slow retreat. His best chance might be to toll Perry into making the first move. If he could counter swiftly enough, maybe he could seize a fractional advantage. Strange to be calculating how he could best smash down the brother he'd idolized. Now Perry was rounding in on him and all Jed's attention tightened on blocking the expected move.

Perry made a sudden rush and uncorked a pulverizing right that Jed avoided partly by dancing back, partly by spinning aside. Even so Perry's fist glanced off his shoulder with a bruising force. But Perry's momentum carried him almost past Jed and as he started to swing back full face, Jed slammed a roundhouse clout to his neck. He heard Perry's pained grunt and fired a second blow, but Perry swiftly hunched his shoulder so that Jed's fist bounced high off his temple.

Ignoring the pain that blazed from his knuckles to his wrist, Jed unhesitatingly followed up, driving his other hand to Perry's chin. The blow snapped Perry's head back an inch or so, but he came piling into Jed with a churning flurry of blows. Jed stepped away from some and parried others, but their driving fury forced him to backpedal so quickly that he lost footing and went sprawling on his back. Perry plunged at him, his boot pulling back for a savage kick. Jed rolled away from it and was already scrambling to his hands and knees as the sweeping miss sent Perry off balance.

Jed came lunging up from the ground, his feet not wholly under him as he made a hurtling dive under Perry's windmilling arms and barreled full into his side, smashing him off his feet. Perry flipped sideways and plunged to the ground like a downed tree. Jed, carried by his awkward momentum, fell half on top of him; Perry tried to grapple. Before he could get a secure grip, Jed pumped two hard straightarm blows into his face, then flung himself away from him.

He watched Perry crawl slowly to his feet, bleeding from the nose and mouth. Jed wasn't hurt, but he rose just as slowly, conserving his strength. The fight could still go either way and Perry was no longer sneering. His eyes gleamed chill blue-green; he'd make no more mistakes, no rash moves.

Jed had no intention of closing with him. Of letting Perry get those big hands on him. Just now Perry was slightly dazed, slowing down somewhat. Jed kept away from him, retreating in a steady circle, moving always backward and sideward, while Perry doggedly stalked him. Perry's temper began to slip; he swore savagely and broke into a floundering run trying to reach Jed. He was tiring quickly now.

Why, Jed thought almost disbelievingly, I can whip him. I can whip Perry! The certain knowledge that the fight was his now gave him an edge of soaring confidence such as he'd never felt.

He shifted to close quarters, drawing a few more wild swings from Perry. These he avoided or knocked aside, meantime hammering Perry around the ribs with short savage blows. He chopped a hard one to the belly; Perry grunted and doubled up, and his whole body seemed to sag. Jed dropped back a step, bracing himself to finish it then and there. In that instant Perry abruptly straightened, his curled right hand whipping up.

Jed saw the blow coming in time to partly deflect it by flinging up his arm. Perry's fist caromed along his skull at an angle. A blow that a man might ordinarily shrug aside. But this one had the impact of a grenade . . .

Jed staggered backward, lights exploding in his head. Beyond a black mist of pain, Perry's face gleamed like a snarling mask. Now Perry's hand was coming up again; this time Jed saw the rock nearly concealed in his fist. The rock he'd quietly scooped up when he had fallen.

He was helpless to dodge or prevent the blow as Perry struck again. Bursting pain and mushrooming darkness. Jed felt the slam of earth against his body. Heard himself groaning as he rolled on his back, spitting dirt. Perry seemed to fill the sky above him, swimming in and out of focus. A hot sourness surged into Jed's throat; he choked on it trying to speak.

Then the blast of a shot filled his ears. The

thunderclap echoes mingled with Perry's shriek. And suddenly Perry was on the ground too, one leg doubled up. He clutched the knee with both hands; blood poured out between his fingers.

Yards away, a man's shape loomed in the raw light. It moved toward them like a rippling shadow. As Jed's eyes began to clear, the shadow assumed solidity and outline.

Aaron Troop stood above them, a rifle in his fist. His eyes were like holes in brown granite. It was he, Jed knew, who had fired the shot.

Chapter 18

Jed got slowly up on one knee. His head was still spinning; he had a hard time focusing on Troop. Dazedly raising a hand to his temple, be found his hair matted with wetness. Perry's blows had split the scalp, but that seemed to be the only damage. He could see Troop's face clearly now and the bleak strangeness of the man's stare sent a chill through him.

But it wasn't at him that Troop was looking. His attention was on Perry, who was clasping his bullet-shattered leg in an agony of shock.

Jed said huskily: "Aaron . . . what are you doing?"

"You don't need to worry about it." Troop's pain-set lips hardly moved; he was swaying like a wind-pressed tree. "You got no mix in this. Stay clear."

"Damn you, Troop . . ." Perry's voice was a painful scraping whisper. "Goddam you to hell. My knee—"

"Smashed all to hell, ain't it? Figured so. Aimed for it."

Jed stared at him in disbelief. "But *why?* Why did you do it?"

"Hell, I figured she'd be ready to leave him if he pushed just a little more. If I could get him to do, that . . ." Troop nodded gently, his eyes squinting almost shut. "Well, it worked, sure enough. She is set to sell TH and leave Starbuck flat. Only she just might take him back sometime. I'd purely hate to see that happen."

A heavy coldness trickled through Jed's stomach. "You mean . . . you did all those things?"

Perry groaned, then slumped in a loose faint. He had passed clean out from the pain.

"Who in hell you think, boy? Only thing

I didn't do was take a shot at him. Hired Bull Jack for that, and he didn't come cheap. Then he had to miss. So I bided my time . . . tried it another way. Better'n killing him. Bust him down, crush his pride, strip him of all he's got. 'Specially her. Yeah. Most of all her . . ."

Troop's voice had begun to fail. He was holding himself tightly erect with an effort. He took his left hand from his rifle and jammed it against his side. His face contorted in a fevered grimace.

Jed inched himself to his feet slowly, slowly. His legs felt rubbery and he had to brace them wide for support. A frown flickered on Troop's face; he snapped the rifle around to bear on Jed. "Boy, you best not move that way again—"

"All right." Jed nodded wearily, as if still dazed from the blow. "Aaron, did you kill those cattle then?"

"Yeah . . . yeah." Troop nodded vaguely, his eyes varnished with pain and fever. "Get him to make a big push against Parral, that would do it, Beth wouldn't take something like that. Well, she didn't. Only what she did do was take over giving orders. But he was still around. She aimed to keep him around . . ."

284

"So you killed Leandro and Poke."

"Wa'n't nothing else I could do. Had to get the crew behind Starbuck against her say-so. No other way to do it. Get him to raid Parral. Maybe kill Parral. Or get hisself killed. Either way he'd be through at TH."

Jed's mind was steadying; his gaze flicked to the coatwrapped guns in the grass a few yards off. "And your hands would be clean. You might even have Beth."

"Yeah . . . yeah." Troop was staring at the unconscious Perry again.

"Only that part didn't work. She didn't turn to you, did she?"

"No," Troop said softly. "She didn't."

"Too bad Perry ever happened along. Things might have been different."

Troop's bloodless face tightened, twitching with hatred. "Yeah," he whispered. "They might of been."

Dawnlight skimmed the slowly lifting barrel of his rifle. His whole attention was on Perry now, on the shame he could wipe out with one bullet.

Jed jackknifed his body as he leaped. Straightened out so that he hit the ground full-length on his belly. Then rolled once, twice, his outflung hand closing over his rolled coat. Dimly he heard Troop shouting. He shook the coat out and grabbed the Army Colt as it fell free. Troop's shot slammed against his eardrums; dirt erupted two feet from his body.

One straining backward roll and he was facing Troop again. Troop was trying to steady his wavering rifle for another shot. Jed thumbed the hammer as he dipped his pistol level and fired. His shot merged with Troop's. This time dirt spewed squarely in his face, blinding him.

One-handed, Jed pawed wildly to clear his eyes. In his other hand the pistol bucked twice more as he fired blindly. Then his eyes were stingingly, wetly clear. White powder-smoke faded and only a pearl sky filled his pistol sights at the end of his extended arm.

He blinked; his eyes swung down. Troop was sprawled and still on his back. He would not move again . . .

The sun was mid-morning high when Jed left the *casa* and got Star from the corral. Then he rode back to the patio where Elizabeth had stepped out to say goodbye. She looked tired, yet her green eyes were alert and serene. Her smile put the grim violence of these past hours gently aside.

"I hope you'll visit us often, you and Elena," she said. "I should think of you together now, shouldn't I?"

He nodded. "That's how it is. But how is it with you now, Beth? You were set on selling out. Leaving TH for good."

"Oh, I don't think so. I don't think so now, Jed."

For a long moment Jed studied her calm lovely face, wondering what had newly developed in back of it. Something had changed for sure. Aaron Troop's bullet had tipped a sudden balance in her life and nothing would be quite the same.

The shots of the fatal exchange behind Troop and him had brought the crew to the spot, but Elizabeth had arrived on the scene well ahead of them. The first shot fired, the one that shattered Perry's knee, had brought her running. She'd given prompt, crisp orders. Still unconscious, Perry had been carried to the house. It would take most of a day to fetch a doctor from Moratown. Elizabeth hadn't organized a nursing society during the war for nothing. Perry's leg would have to come off, that was certain. Jed, after one look at the pulpy horror of bone splinters and mangled flesh that had been a knee, had queasily agreed. Amputation was the common remedy for such, and several crewmen as well as Elizabeth herself were familiar with details of primitive surgery.

It had been done. Perry was still deep in opiates and Jed didn't want to be here when he came to his senses. Besides Elena would be waiting for news. And there was no more to be done here. But how things would turn out with Perry weighed heavily on his mind.

Elizabeth echoed the thought.

"I think that things will be different now," she said. "Quite a bit different, Jed."

He nodded, feeling a little puzzled. Of course Perry would need care and help; any dutiful wife would stand by a man in his need. But Elizabeth didn't appear to regret the prospect. Quite the contrary. Maybe he was wrong, but her manner almost seemed one of tranquil satisfaction.

A smile ghosted at the corners of her mouth. "We're all family, remember? We'll be expecting you to visit often."

Yes, things would be different. For by now she knew Perry well. Knew how closely his personal pride of strength had been knit to his physical prowess. To the native abilities which had enabled him to do nearly anything faster and better than other men. No way as yet to wholly measure what the bullet that had shattered his knee had done to his spirit, his ambitions, his driving force. But knowing Perry, Jed had a firm premonition about it.

And looking at Elizabeth in this moment, he had another. Hers would now be the ascendant, the dominant voice. She had been handed the means to control Perry and the sure, triumphant knowledge of it glinted behind her calm. Hard now to believe that Elizabeth Hobart Starbuck had ever been less than what she indisputably was: chatelaine and mistress of her home and her lands.

Jed touched his hat. "Good luck, Beth."

As he rode away from TH, he had the wry thought that it was Perry who would need the luck. All of it he could get.

And himself? He had all that he needed, Jed believed. For he knew where he was going. Elena's horse, ears pointed forward as he moved strongly and steadily into the growing day, knew it too. Home.